TOP SECRET GRAPHICA MYSTERIES

CASEBOOK: BIGFOOT

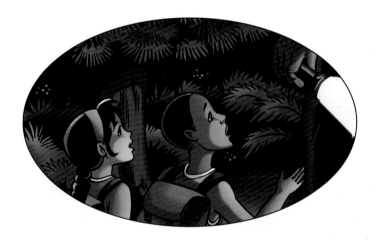

Script by Justine and Ron Fontes

Layouts and Designs by Ron Fontes

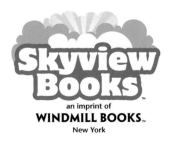

Skyview Books™

an imprint of

WINDMILL BOOKS™

New York

Published in 2010 by Windmill Books, LLC
303 Park Avenue South, Suite # 1280
New York, NY 10010-3657

CREDITS:
Script by Justine and Ron Fontes
Layouts and designs by Ron Fontes
Art by Planman, Ltd.

Publisher Cataloging in Publication

Fontes, Justine
        Casebook--Bigfoot. – School and library ed. / script by Justine and Ron Fontes;
layouts and designs by Ron Fontes; art by Planman, Ltd.
p.   cm. – (Top secret graphica mysteries)
Summary: When Tracy's video wins her the opportunity to be Mr. Mystery's
junior reporter, she and her friends set out on an adventure in Bigfoot country.
ISBN 978-1-60754-594-1 – ISBN 978-1-60754-595-8 (pbk.)
ISBN 978-1-60754-596-5 (6-pack)
        1. Sasquatch—Juvenile fiction   2. Graphic novels   [1. Sasquatch—Fiction
2. Reporters and reporting—Fiction   3. Graphic novels]   I. Fontes, Ron   II. Title
III. Title: Bigfoot   IV. Series
        741.5/973—dc22

Manufactured in the United States of America

CONTENTS

Welcome to the Windmill Bakery

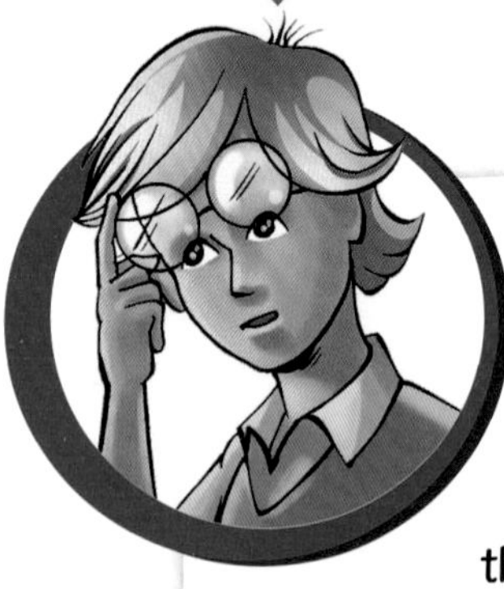

Edward Icarus Stein is known as "Einstein" because of his initials "E.I." and his last name, and because he loves science the way fanatical fans love sports. Einstein dedicates his waking hours to observing as much as he can of all the strange things just beyond human knowledge, because "that's the discovery zone," as he calls it. Einstein aspires to nothing less than living up to his nickname and coming up with a truly groundbreaking scientific discovery. So far this brilliant seventh grader's best invention is the Virtual Visors he and his friends use to explore strange phenomena. Einstein's parents own the local bakery where the friends meet.

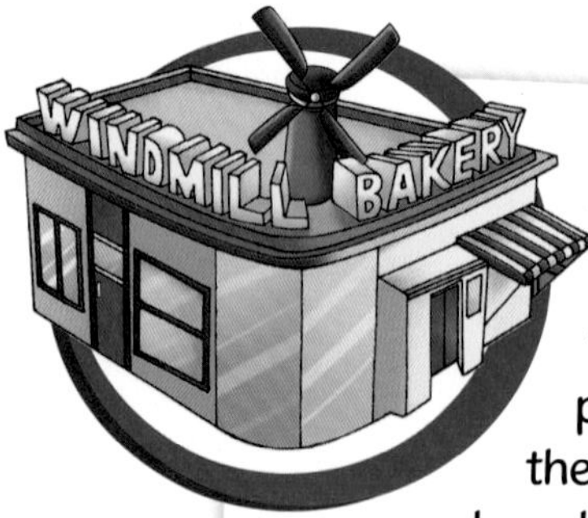
WINDMILL
BAKERY

The Windmill Bakery is a cozy place where friends and neighbors buy homemade goodies to go or to eat on the premises. Einstein's kindhearted parents make everyone feel welcome, especially the friends who understand their exceptional son and share his appetite for discovery!

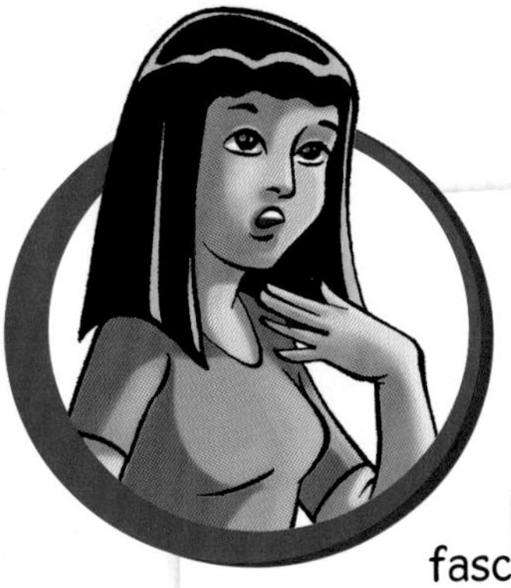

"Spacey Tracy" Lee saw a UFO when she was seven. Her parents tried to dismiss the incident as a "waking dream." But Tracy knew what she saw and it inspired her to investigate the UFO phenomenon. The more she learned, the more fascinated she became. She earned her nickname by constantly talking about UFOs. Tracy hopes to become a reporter when she grows up so she can continue to explore the unknown. A straight-A student, Tracy enjoys swimming, gymnastics, and playing the cello. Now that she's "more mature" and hoping to lose the silly nickname, Tracy shares the experience that changed her life forever only with her Virtual Visor buddies.

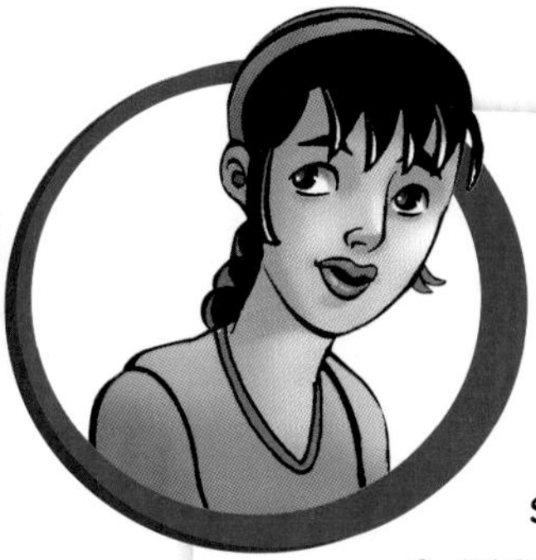

Clarita Gonzales knows that Indiana Jones and Lara Croft aren't real people, but that doesn't stop this seventh grader from wanting to be an adventurous archaeologist. Clarita's parents will support any path she chooses, as long as she gets a good education. Unfortunately, school isn't her strong point. During most classes, Clarita's mind wanders to, as she puts it, "more exciting places—like Atlantis!" A tomboy thanks to her three older brothers and one younger brother, Clarita is a great soccer player and is also into martial arts. Her interest in archaeology extends to architecture, artifacts, cooking, and all forms of culture. (Clarita would have a crush on Einstein if he wasn't "such a bookworm")!

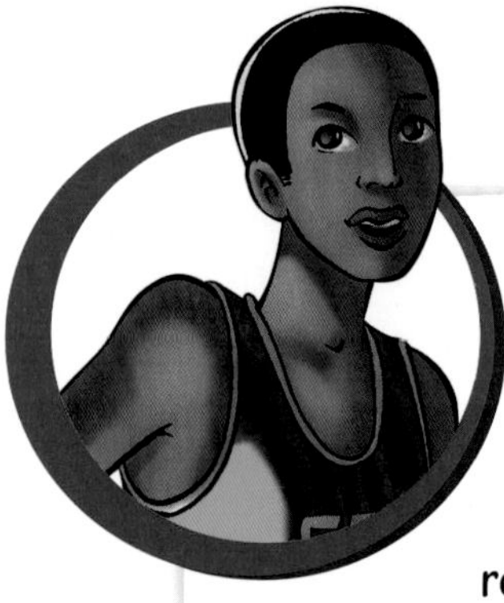

"Freaky Frank" Phillips earned his nickname because of his uncanny ability to use his "extra senses," a "gift" he inherited from his grandma. Though this eighth grader can't predict the winners of the next SUPERBOWL (or, he admits, "anything really useful"), Frank "knows" when someone is lying or otherwise up to no good. He gets "warnings" before trouble strikes. And sometimes he "sees things that aren't there"—at least to those less sensitive to things like auras and ghosts. Frank isn't sure what he wants to be when he grows up. He enjoys keeping tropical fish and does well in every subject, except math. "Numbers make my head hurt," Frank confesses. Frank spends lots of time with his family and his fish, but he's always up for an adventure with his friends.

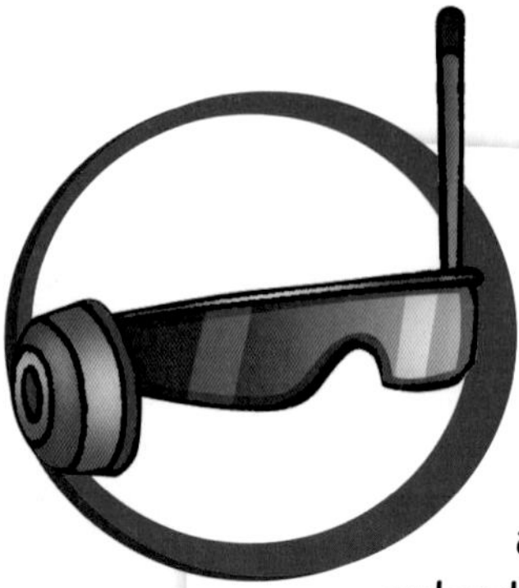

The Virtual Visors allow Einstein, Frank, Clarita, and Tracy to pursue their taste for adventure well beyond the boundaries of the bakery. Thanks to Einstein's brilliant software, the visors can simulate all kinds of locations and experiences based on the uploaded facts. Once inside the program, the visors become invisible. When danger gets too intense, the kids can always touch their Virtual Visors to return to the bakery. Sometimes the kids explore in the real world without the visors. But more often they use these devices to explore the mysteries and phenomena that intrigue each member of the group. The Virtual Visors are the ultimate virtual reality research tool, even though you never know what quirky things might happen thanks to Einstein's "Random Adventure Program."

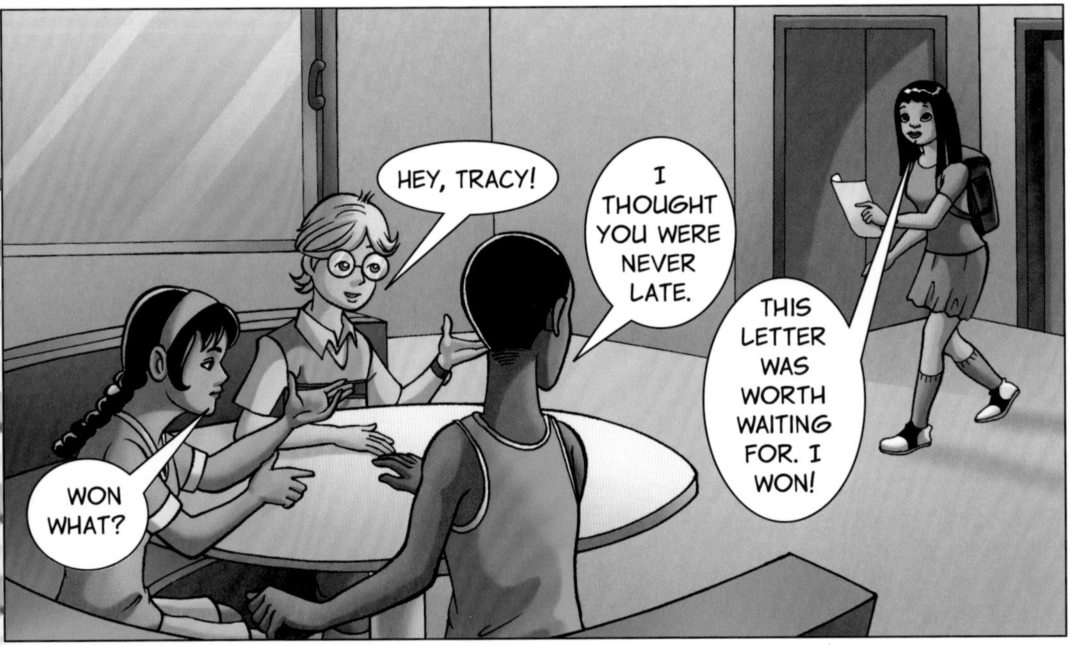
HEY, TRACY!
I THOUGHT YOU WERE NEVER LATE.
THIS LETTER WAS WORTH WAITING FOR. I WON!
WON WHAT?

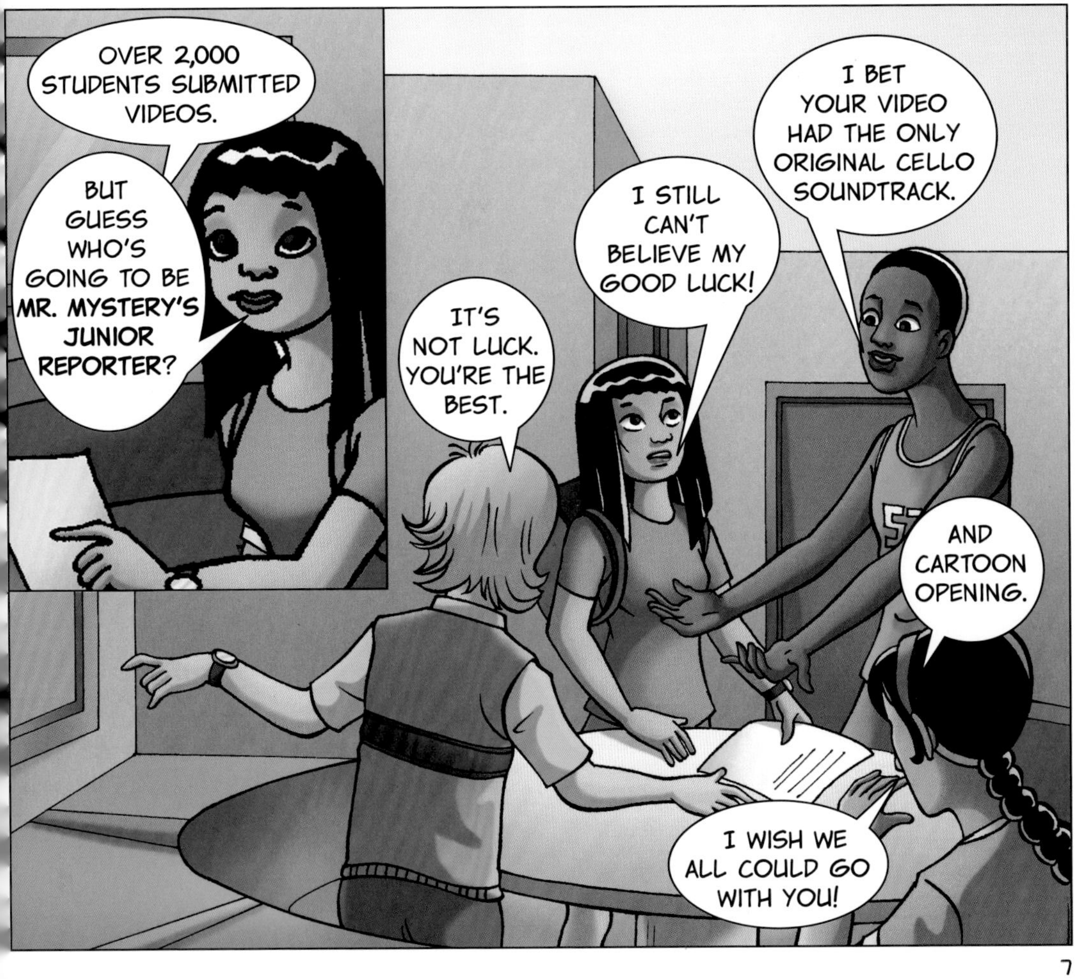
OVER 2,000 STUDENTS SUBMITTED VIDEOS.
BUT GUESS WHO'S GOING TO BE **MR. MYSTERY'S JUNIOR** REPORTER?
I BET YOUR VIDEO HAD THE ONLY ORIGINAL CELLO SOUNDTRACK.
I STILL CAN'T BELIEVE MY GOOD LUCK!
IT'S NOT LUCK. YOU'RE THE BEST.
AND CARTOON OPENING.
I WISH WE ALL COULD GO WITH YOU!

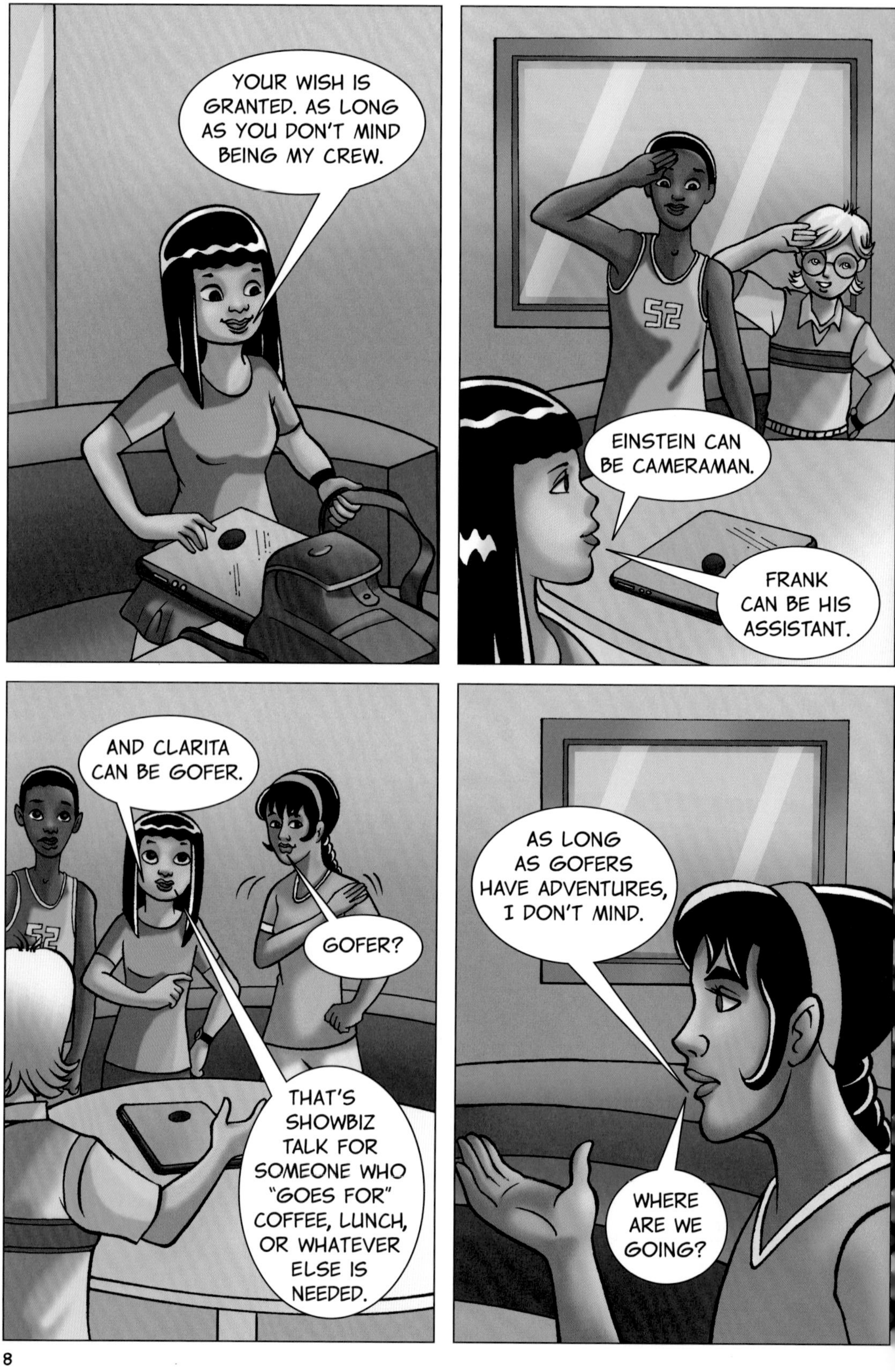
YOUR WISH IS GRANTED. AS LONG AS YOU DON'T MIND BEING MY CREW.
EINSTEIN CAN BE CAMERAMAN.
FRANK CAN BE HIS ASSISTANT.
AND CLARITA CAN BE GOFER.
GOFER?
THAT'S SHOWBIZ TALK FOR SOMEONE WHO "GOES FOR" COFFEE, LUNCH, OR WHATEVER ELSE IS NEEDED.
AS LONG AS GOFERS HAVE ADVENTURES, I DON'T MIND.
WHERE ARE WE GOING?

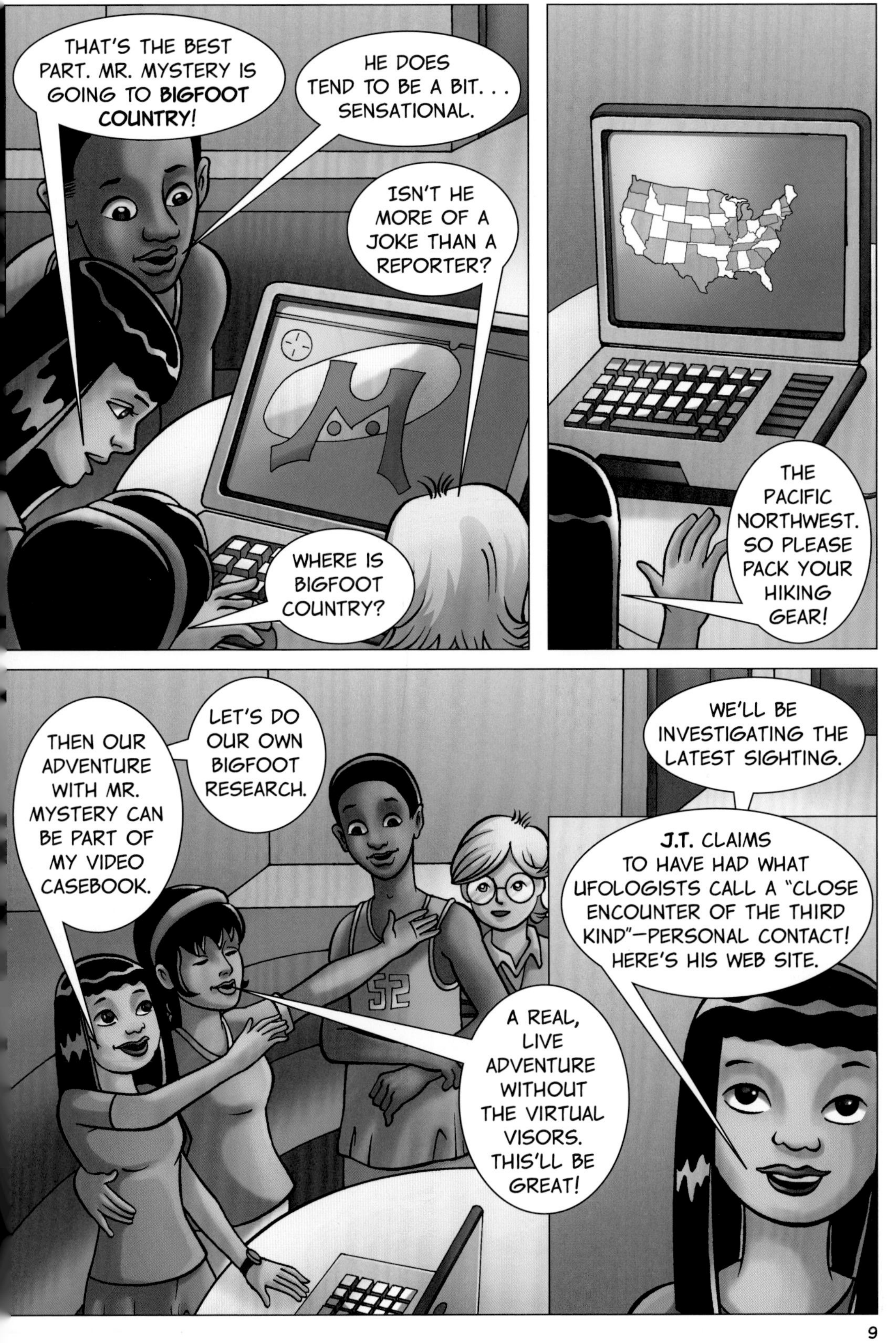
THAT'S THE BEST PART. MR. MYSTERY IS GOING TO BIGFOOT COUNTRY!
HE DOES TEND TO BE A BIT. . . SENSATIONAL.
ISN'T HE MORE OF A JOKE THAN A REPORTER?
WHERE IS BIGFOOT COUNTRY?
THE PACIFIC NORTHWEST. SO PLEASE PACK YOUR HIKING GEAR!
THEN OUR ADVENTURE WITH MR. MYSTERY CAN BE PART OF MY VIDEO CASEBOOK.
LET'S DO OUR OWN BIGFOOT RESEARCH.
A REAL, LIVE ADVENTURE WITHOUT THE VIRTUAL VISORS. THIS'LL BE GREAT!
WE'LL BE INVESTIGATING THE LATEST SIGHTING.
J.T. CLAIMS TO HAVE HAD WHAT UFOLOGISTS CALL A "CLOSE ENCOUNTER OF THE THIRD KIND"—PERSONAL CONTACT! HERE'S HIS WEB SITE.

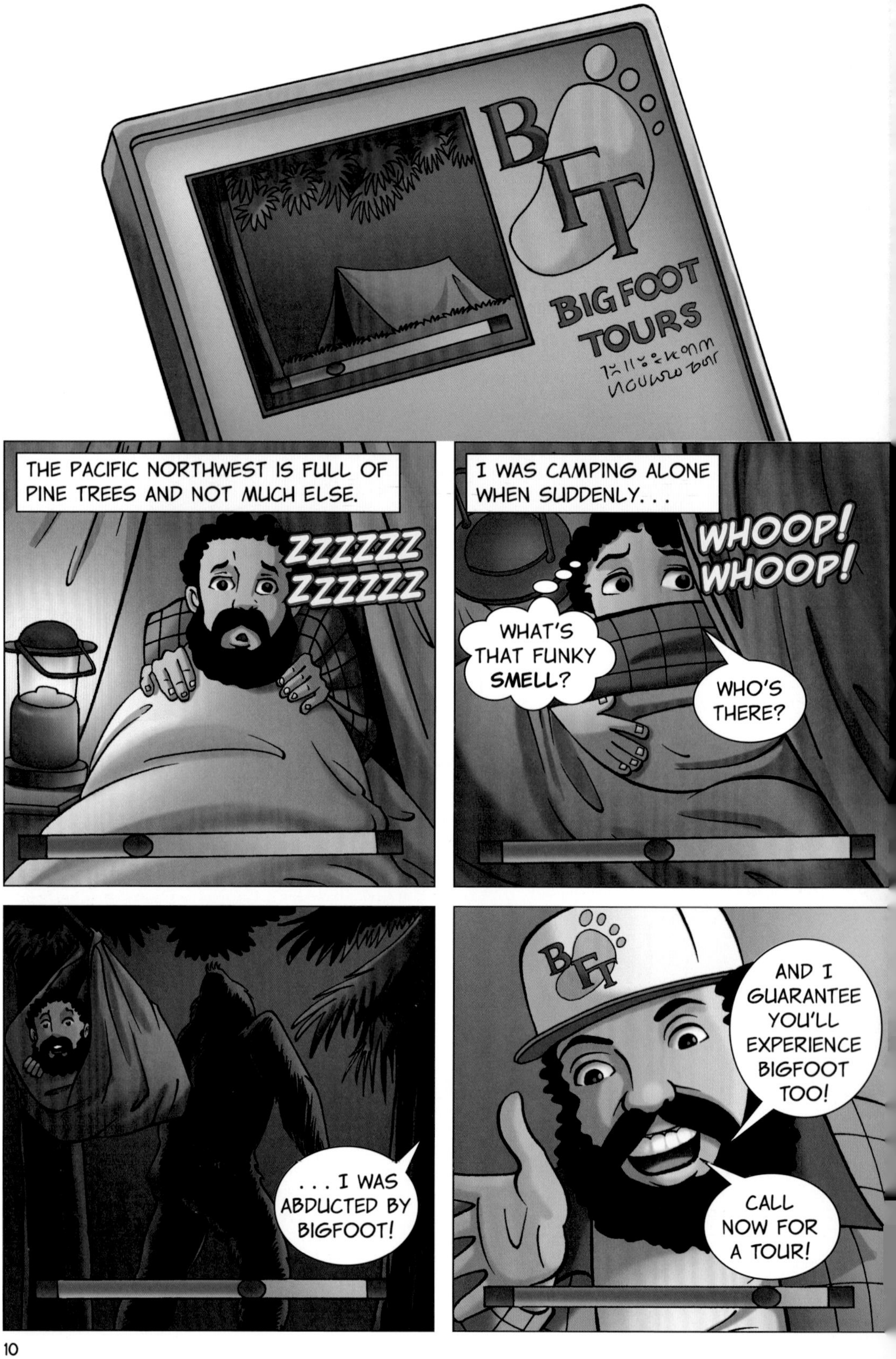
BFT
BIGFOOT TOURS
THE PACIFIC NORTHWEST IS FULL OF PINE TREES AND NOT MUCH ELSE.
ZZZZZZ ZZZZZZ
I WAS CAMPING ALONE WHEN SUDDENLY. . .
WHOOP! WHOOP!
WHAT'S THAT FUNKY SMELL?
WHO'S THERE?
. . . I WAS ABDUCTED BY BIGFOOT!
BFT
AND I GUARANTEE YOU'LL EXPERIENCE BIGFOOT TOO!
CALL NOW FOR A TOUR!

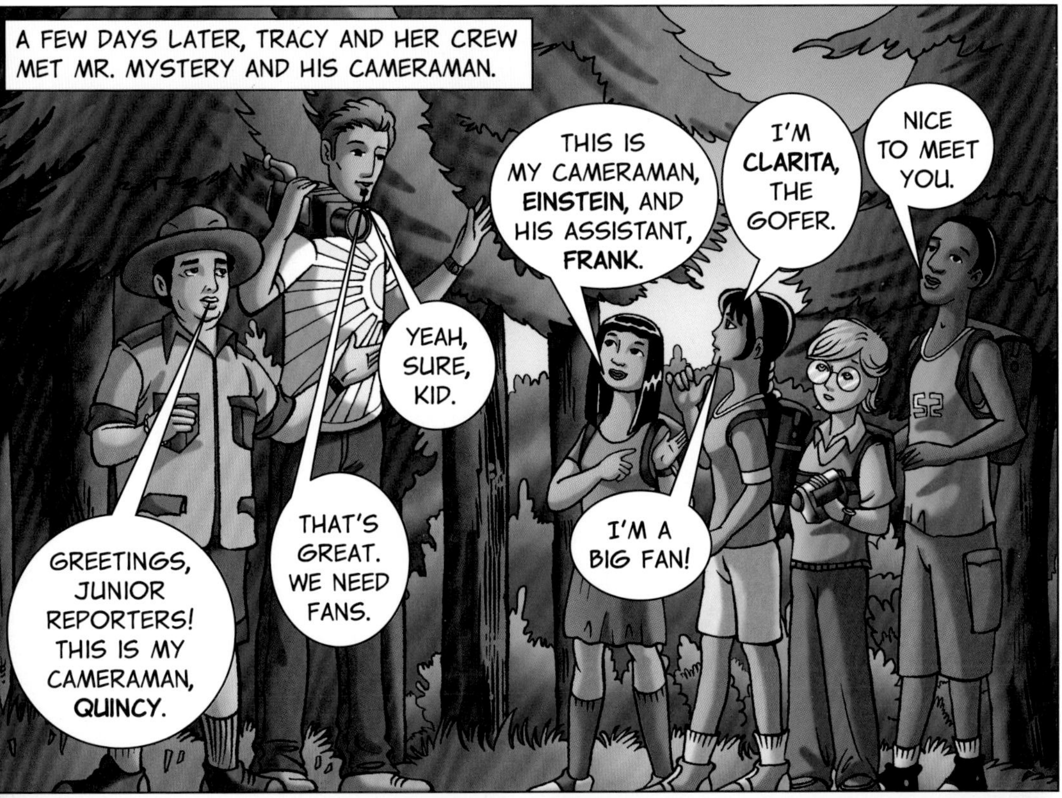
A FEW DAYS LATER, TRACY AND HER CREW MET MR. MYSTERY AND HIS CAMERAMAN.
GREETINGS, JUNIOR REPORTERS! THIS IS MY CAMERAMAN, **QUINCY**.
YEAH, SURE, KID.
THIS IS MY CAMERAMAN, **EINSTEIN,** AND HIS ASSISTANT, **FRANK.**
I'M **CLARITA,** THE GOFER.
NICE TO MEET YOU.
I'M A BIG FAN!
THAT'S GREAT. WE NEED FANS.

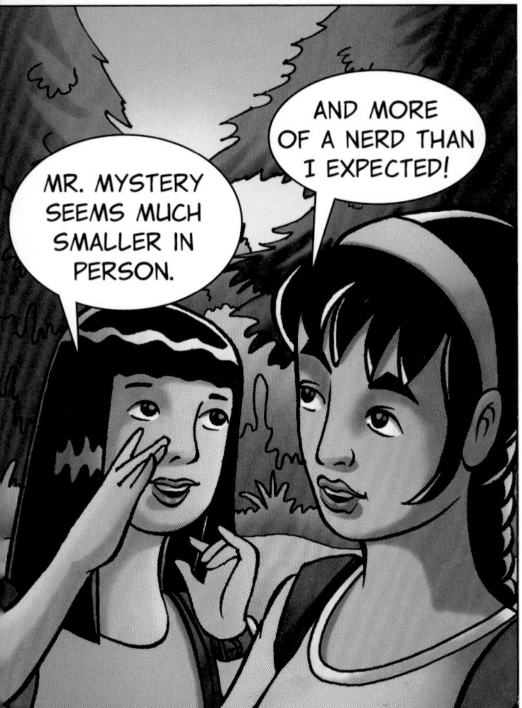
MR. MYSTERY SEEMS MUCH SMALLER IN PERSON.
AND MORE OF A NERD THAN I EXPECTED!

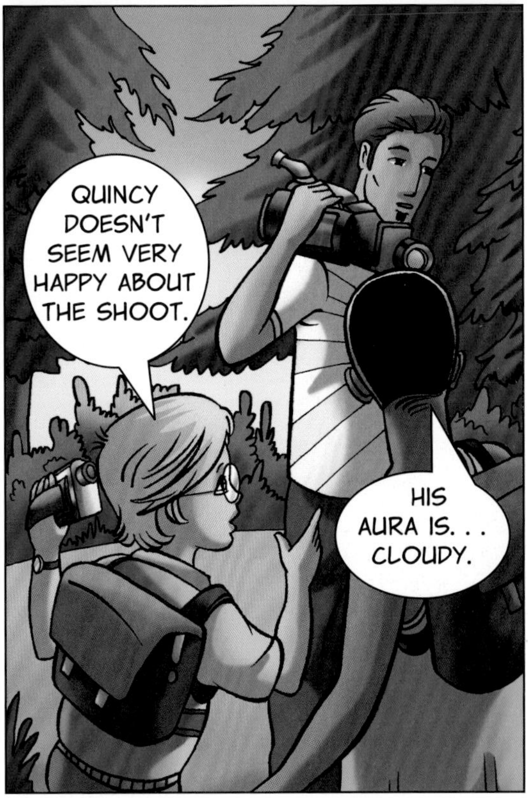
QUINCY DOESN'T SEEM VERY HAPPY ABOUT THE SHOOT.
HIS AURA IS. . . CLOUDY.

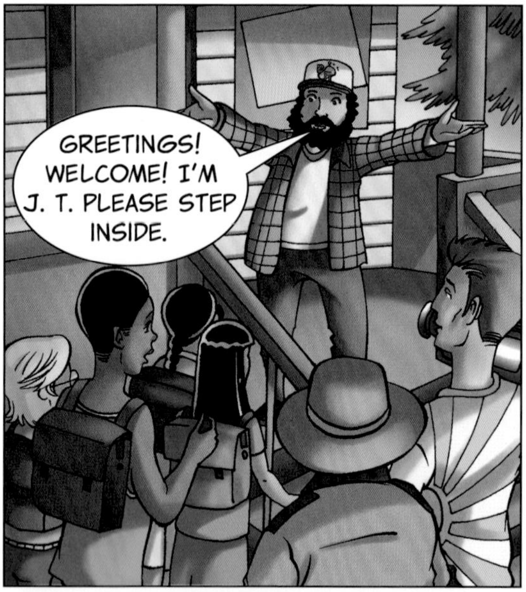
GREETINGS! WELCOME! I'M J. T. PLEASE STEP INSIDE.

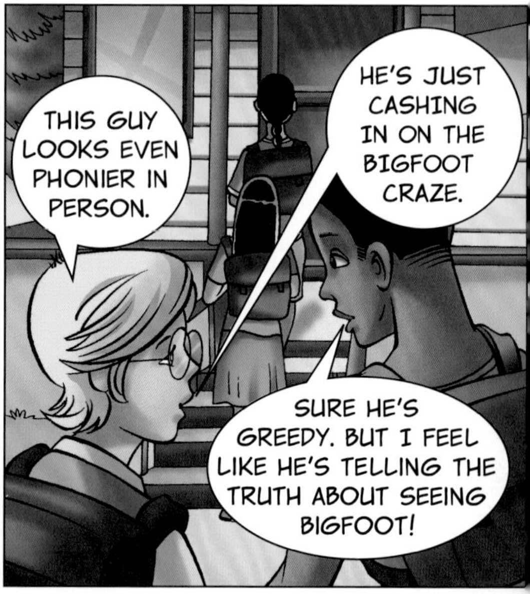
THIS GUY LOOKS EVEN PHONIER IN PERSON.
HE'S JUST CASHING IN ON THE BIGFOOT CRAZE.
SURE HE'S GREEDY. BUT I FEEL LIKE HE'S TELLING THE TRUTH ABOUT SEEING BIGFOOT!

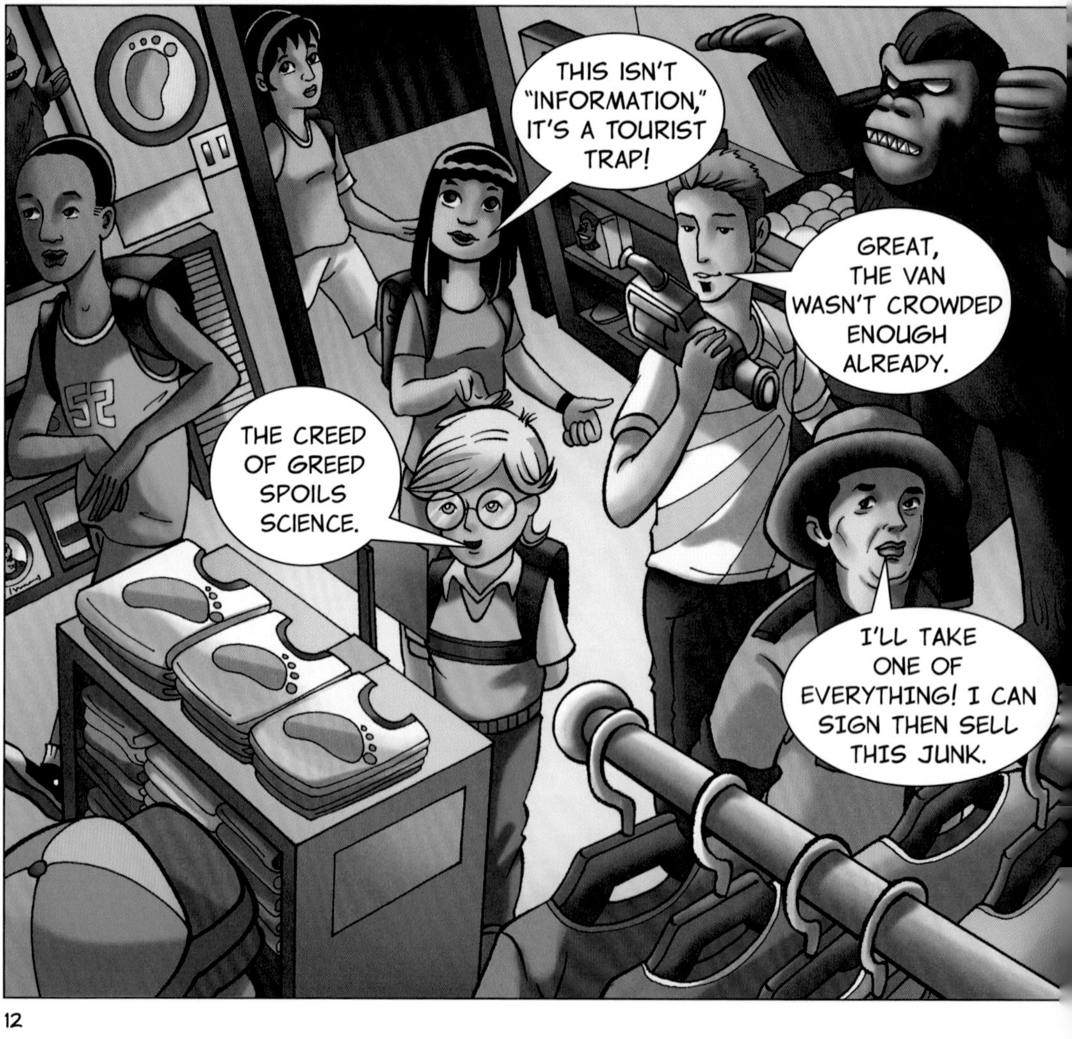
THIS ISN'T "INFORMATION," IT'S A TOURIST TRAP!
GREAT, THE VAN WASN'T CROWDED ENOUGH ALREADY.
THE CREED OF GREED SPOILS SCIENCE.
I'LL TAKE ONE OF EVERYTHING! I CAN SIGN THEN SELL THIS JUNK.

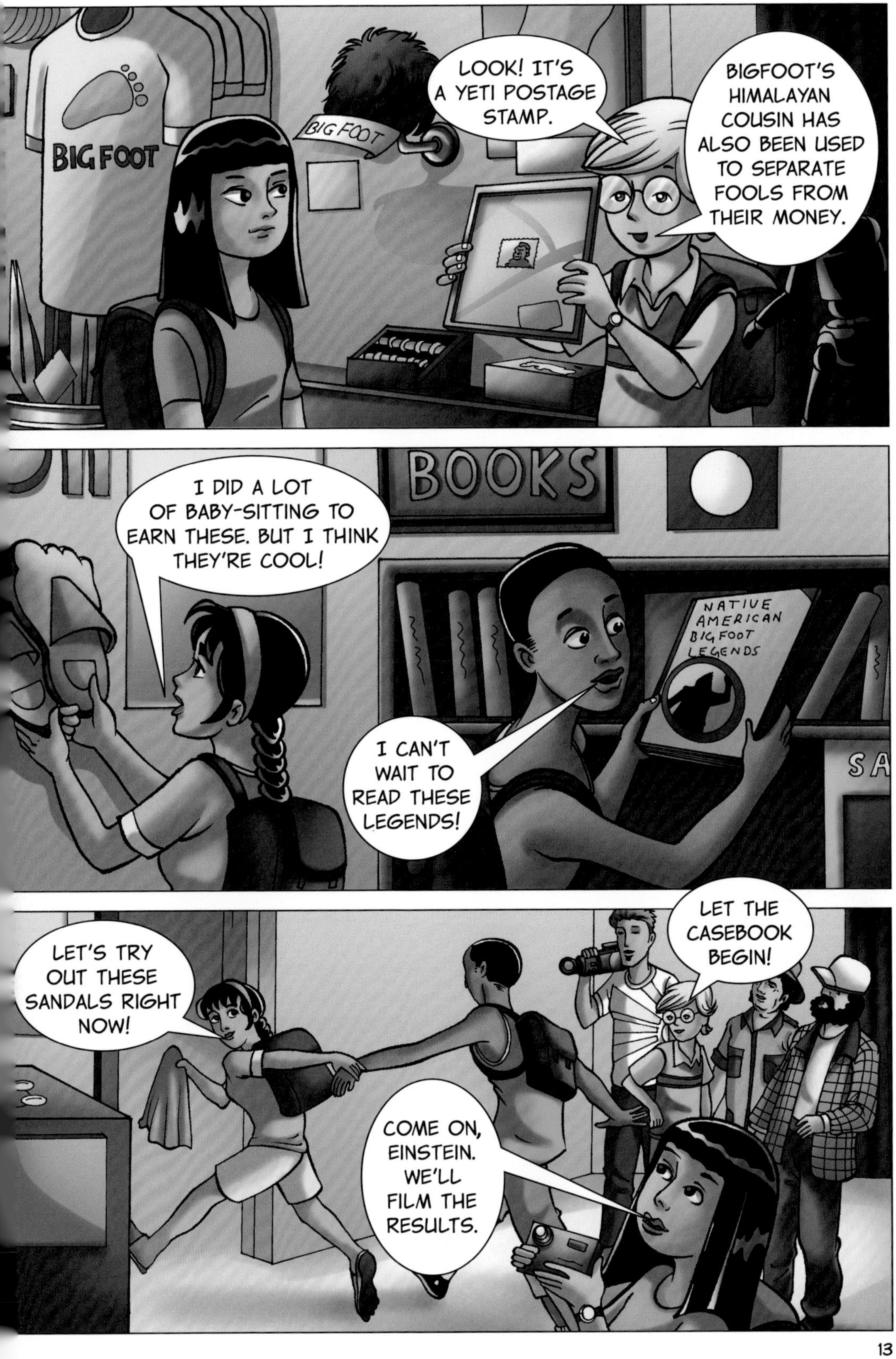
BIG FOOT
BIGFOOT
LOOK! IT'S A YETI POSTAGE STAMP.
BIGFOOT'S HIMALAYAN COUSIN HAS ALSO BEEN USED TO SEPARATE FOOLS FROM THEIR MONEY.
BOOKS
I DID A LOT OF BABY-SITTING TO EARN THESE. BUT I THINK THEY'RE COOL!
NATIVE AMERICAN BIGFOOT LEGENDS
I CAN'T WAIT TO READ THESE LEGENDS!
LET'S TRY OUT THESE SANDALS RIGHT NOW!
LET THE CASEBOOK BEGIN!
COME ON, EINSTEIN. WE'LL FILM THE RESULTS.

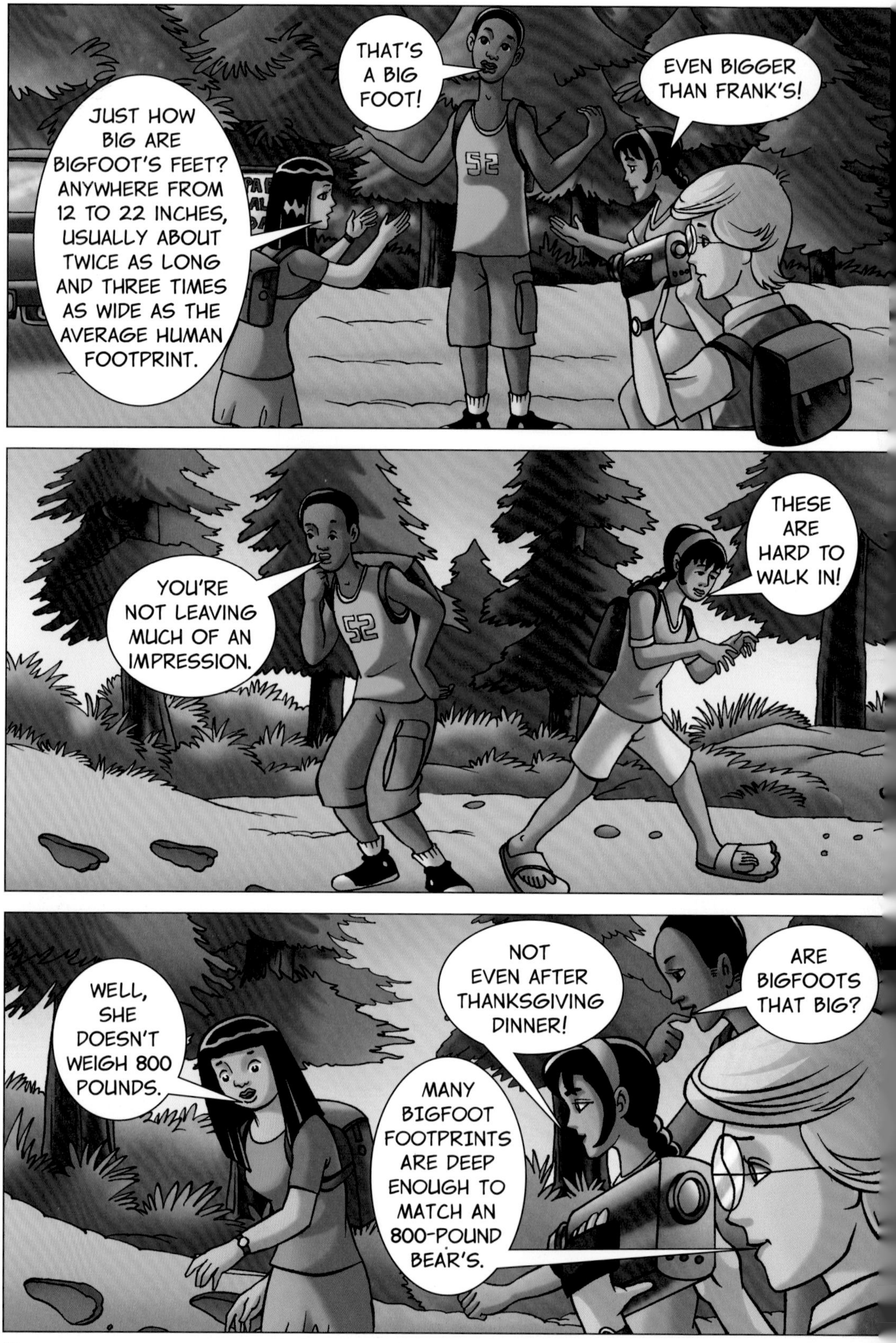
JUST HOW BIG ARE BIGFOOT'S FEET? ANYWHERE FROM 12 TO 22 INCHES, USUALLY ABOUT TWICE AS LONG AND THREE TIMES AS WIDE AS THE AVERAGE HUMAN FOOTPRINT.
THAT'S A BIG FOOT!
EVEN BIGGER THAN FRANK'S!
YOU'RE NOT LEAVING MUCH OF AN IMPRESSION.
THESE ARE HARD TO WALK IN!
WELL, SHE DOESN'T WEIGH 800 POUNDS.
NOT EVEN AFTER THANKSGIVING DINNER!
ARE BIGFOOTS THAT BIG?
MANY BIGFOOT FOOTPRINTS ARE DEEP ENOUGH TO MATCH AN 800-POUND BEAR'S.

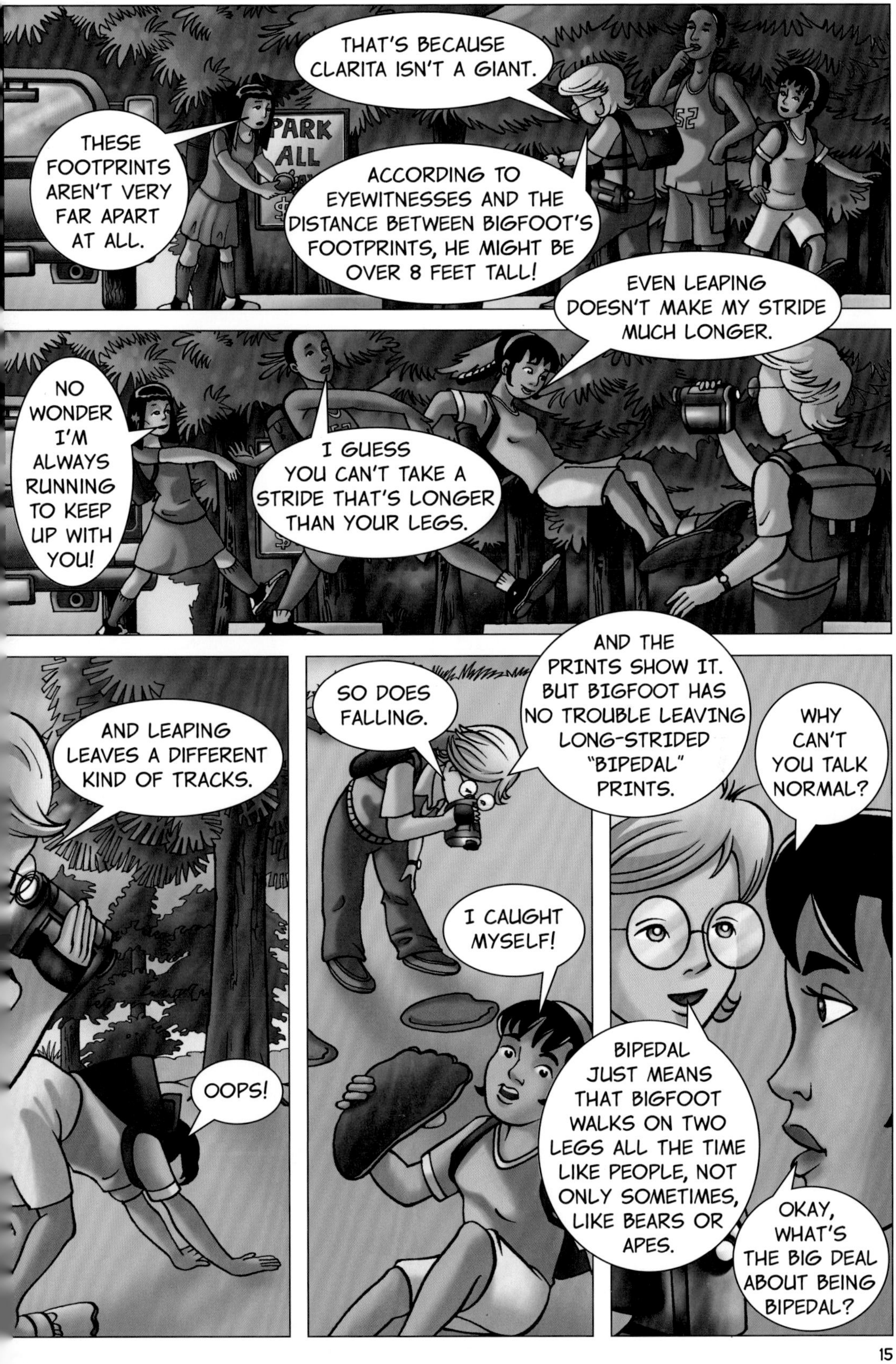

THESE FOOTPRINTS AREN'T VERY FAR APART AT ALL.
THAT'S BECAUSE CLARITA ISN'T A GIANT.
ACCORDING TO EYEWITNESSES AND THE DISTANCE BETWEEN BIGFOOT'S FOOTPRINTS, HE MIGHT BE OVER 8 FEET TALL!
PARK ALL
EVEN LEAPING DOESN'T MAKE MY STRIDE MUCH LONGER.
NO WONDER I'M ALWAYS RUNNING TO KEEP UP WITH YOU!
I GUESS YOU CAN'T TAKE A STRIDE THAT'S LONGER THAN YOUR LEGS.
AND LEAPING LEAVES A DIFFERENT KIND OF TRACKS.
OOPS!
SO DOES FALLING.
AND THE PRINTS SHOW IT. BUT BIGFOOT HAS NO TROUBLE LEAVING LONG-STRIDED "BIPEDAL" PRINTS.
I CAUGHT MYSELF!
WHY CAN'T YOU TALK NORMAL?
BIPEDAL JUST MEANS THAT BIGFOOT WALKS ON TWO LEGS ALL THE TIME LIKE PEOPLE, NOT ONLY SOMETIMES, LIKE BEARS OR APES.
OKAY, WHAT'S THE BIG DEAL ABOUT BEING BIPEDAL?

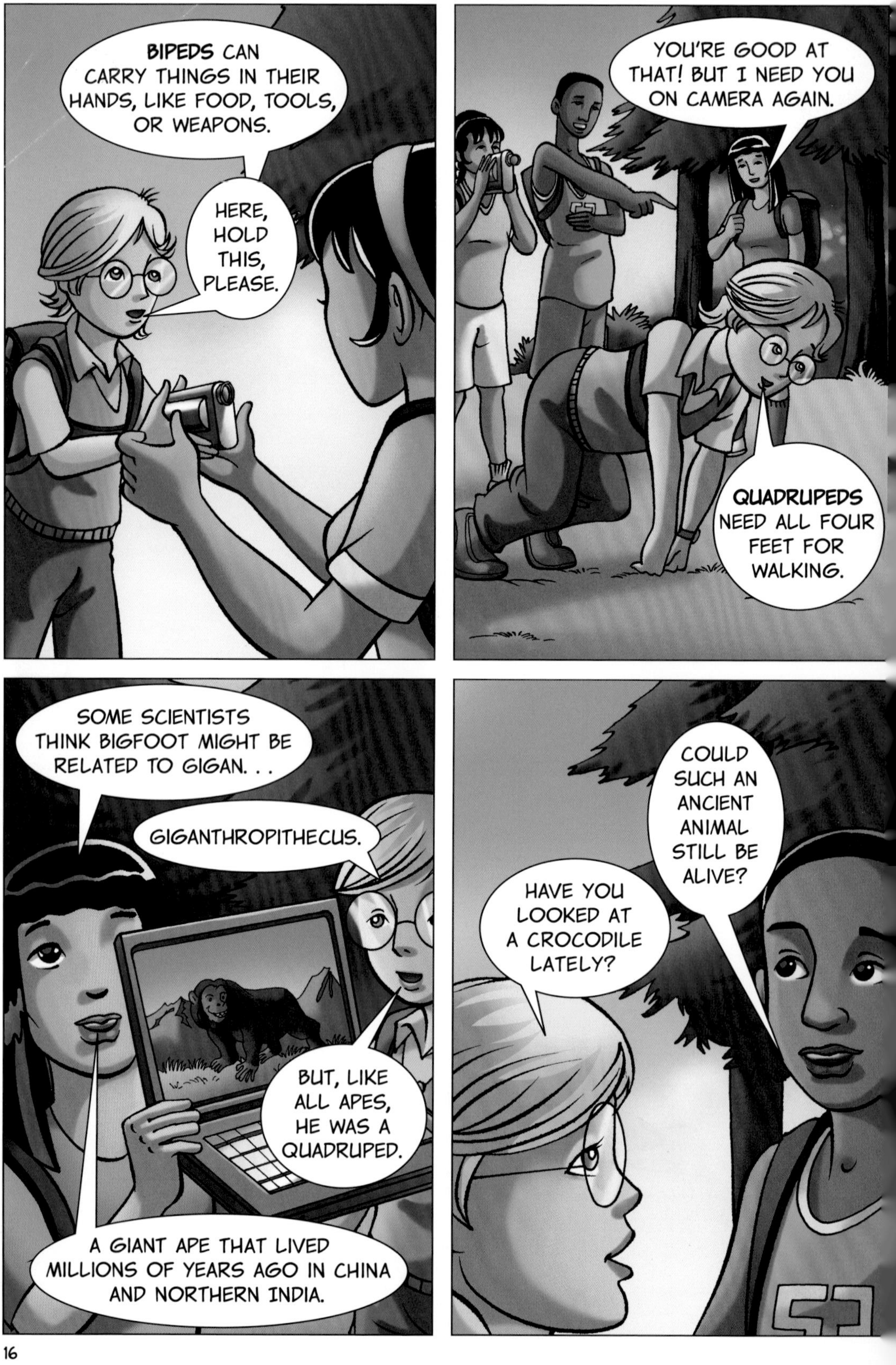
BIPEDS CAN CARRY THINGS IN THEIR HANDS, LIKE FOOD, TOOLS, OR WEAPONS.
HERE, HOLD THIS, PLEASE.
YOU'RE GOOD AT THAT! BUT I NEED YOU ON CAMERA AGAIN.
QUADRUPEDS NEED ALL FOUR FEET FOR WALKING.
SOME SCIENTISTS THINK BIGFOOT MIGHT BE RELATED TO GIGAN. . .
GIGANTHROPITHECUS.
A GIANT APE THAT LIVED MILLIONS OF YEARS AGO IN CHINA AND NORTHERN INDIA.
BUT, LIKE ALL APES, HE WAS A QUADRUPED.
COULD SUCH AN ANCIENT ANIMAL STILL BE ALIVE?
HAVE YOU LOOKED AT A CROCODILE LATELY?

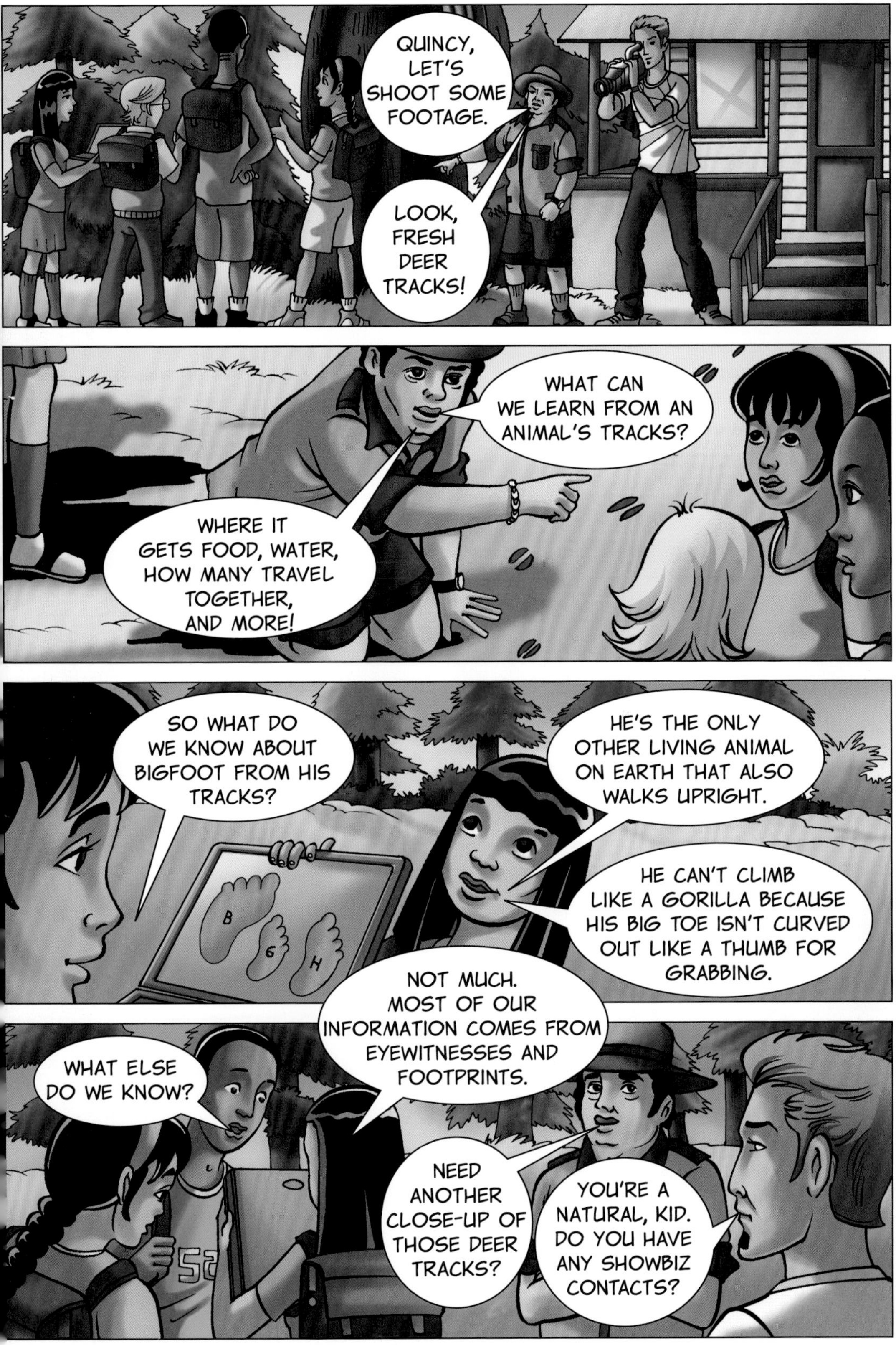
QUINCY, LET'S SHOOT SOME FOOTAGE.
LOOK, FRESH DEER TRACKS!
WHAT CAN WE LEARN FROM AN ANIMAL'S TRACKS?
WHERE IT GETS FOOD, WATER, HOW MANY TRAVEL TOGETHER, AND MORE!
SO WHAT DO WE KNOW ABOUT BIGFOOT FROM HIS TRACKS?
HE'S THE ONLY OTHER LIVING ANIMAL ON EARTH THAT ALSO WALKS UPRIGHT.
HE CAN'T CLIMB LIKE A GORILLA BECAUSE HIS BIG TOE ISN'T CURVED OUT LIKE A THUMB FOR GRABBING.
WHAT ELSE DO WE KNOW?
NOT MUCH. MOST OF OUR INFORMATION COMES FROM EYEWITNESSES AND FOOTPRINTS.
NEED ANOTHER CLOSE-UP OF THOSE DEER TRACKS?
YOU'RE A NATURAL, KID. DO YOU HAVE ANY SHOWBIZ CONTACTS?

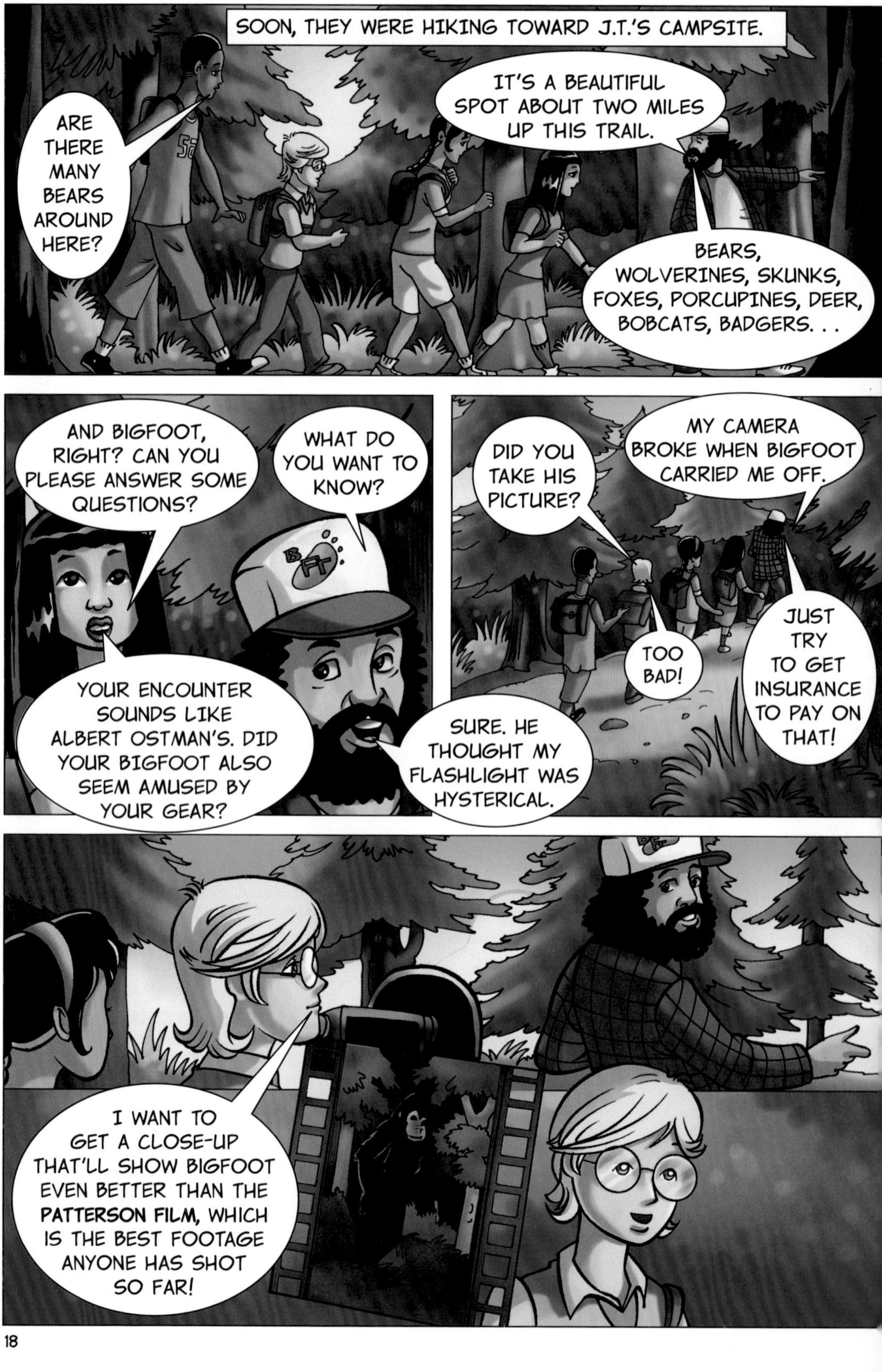

SOON, THEY WERE HIKING TOWARD J.T.'S CAMPSITE.
ARE THERE MANY BEARS AROUND HERE?
IT'S A BEAUTIFUL SPOT ABOUT TWO MILES UP THIS TRAIL.
BEARS, WOLVERINES, SKUNKS, FOXES, PORCUPINES, DEER, BOBCATS, BADGERS. . .
AND BIGFOOT, RIGHT? CAN YOU PLEASE ANSWER SOME QUESTIONS?
WHAT DO YOU WANT TO KNOW?
YOUR ENCOUNTER SOUNDS LIKE ALBERT OSTMAN'S. DID YOUR BIGFOOT ALSO SEEM AMUSED BY YOUR GEAR?
SURE. HE THOUGHT MY FLASHLIGHT WAS HYSTERICAL.
DID YOU TAKE HIS PICTURE?
MY CAMERA BROKE WHEN BIGFOOT CARRIED ME OFF.
TOO BAD!
JUST TRY TO GET INSURANCE TO PAY ON THAT!
I WANT TO GET A CLOSE-UP THAT'LL SHOW BIGFOOT EVEN BETTER THAN THE **PATTERSON FILM,** WHICH IS THE BEST FOOTAGE ANYONE HAS SHOT SO FAR!

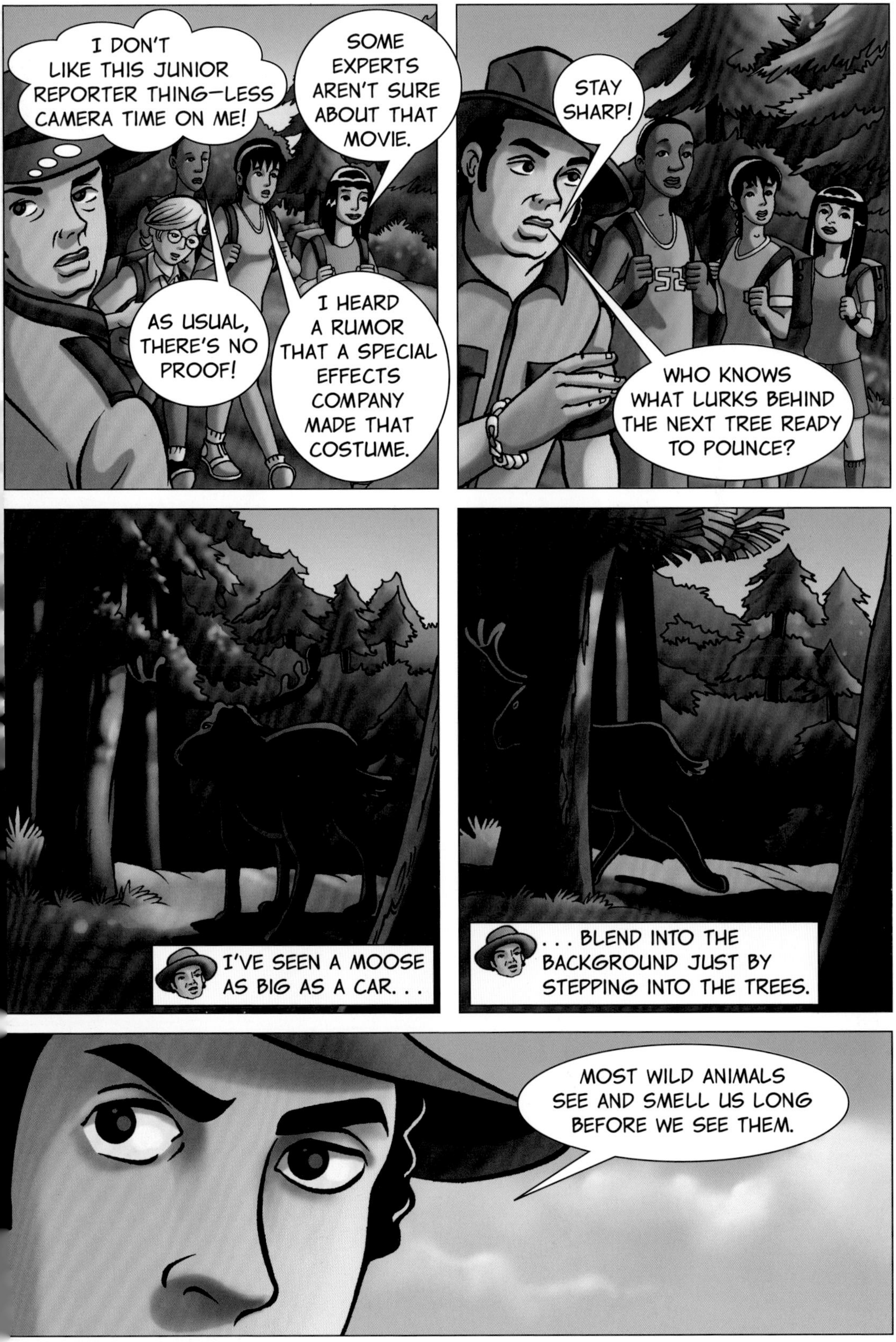
I DON'T LIKE THIS JUNIOR REPORTER THING—LESS CAMERA TIME ON ME!
SOME EXPERTS AREN'T SURE ABOUT THAT MOVIE.
AS USUAL, THERE'S NO PROOF!
I HEARD A RUMOR THAT A SPECIAL EFFECTS COMPANY MADE THAT COSTUME.
STAY SHARP!
WHO KNOWS WHAT LURKS BEHIND THE NEXT TREE READY TO POUNCE?
I'VE SEEN A MOOSE AS BIG AS A CAR. . .
. . . BLEND INTO THE BACKGROUND JUST BY STEPPING INTO THE TREES.
MOST WILD ANIMALS SEE AND SMELL US LONG BEFORE WE SEE THEM.

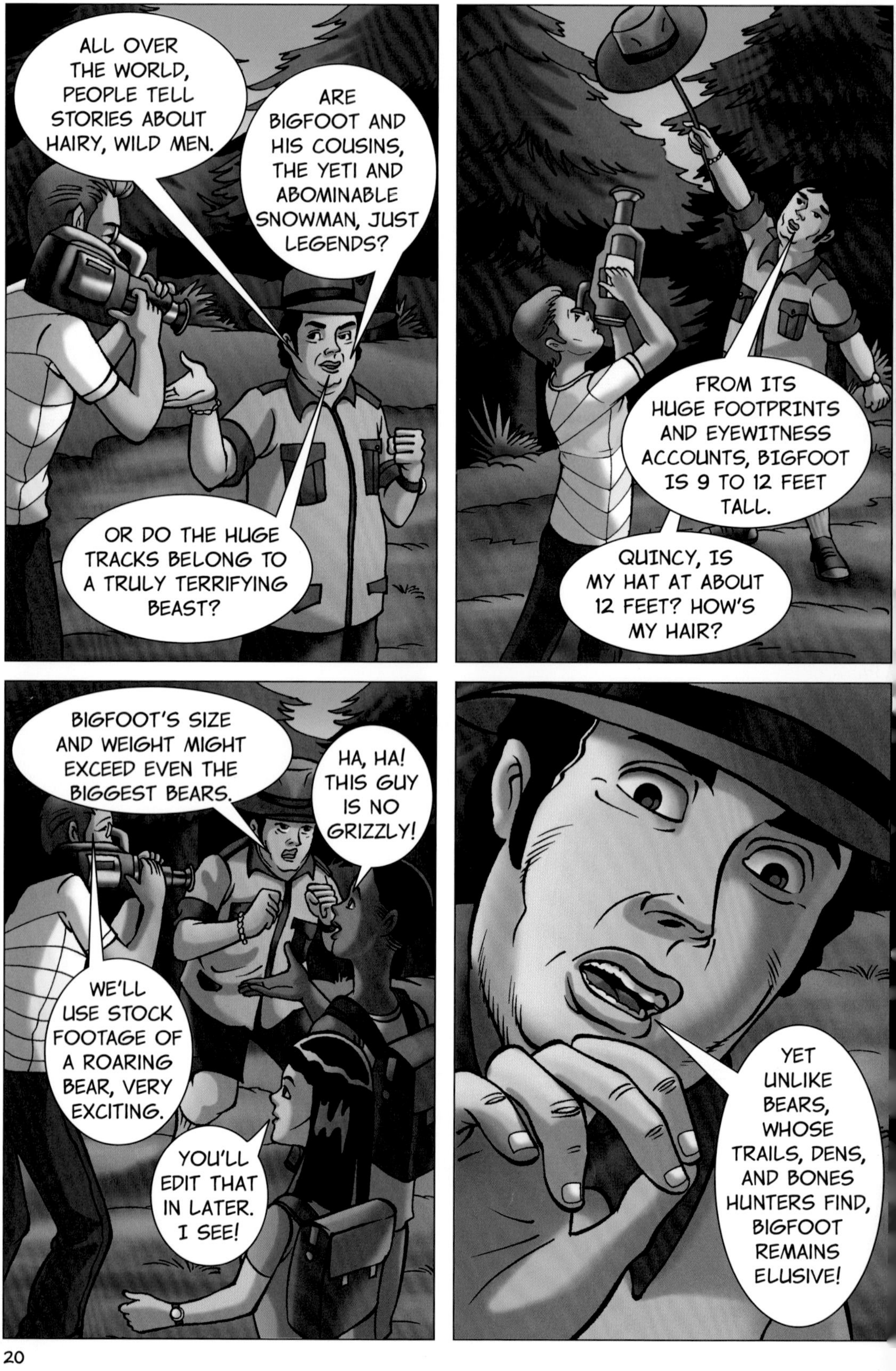
ALL OVER THE WORLD, PEOPLE TELL STORIES ABOUT HAIRY, WILD MEN.
ARE BIGFOOT AND HIS COUSINS, THE YETI AND ABOMINABLE SNOWMAN, JUST LEGENDS?
OR DO THE HUGE TRACKS BELONG TO A TRULY TERRIFYING BEAST?
FROM ITS HUGE FOOTPRINTS AND EYEWITNESS ACCOUNTS, BIGFOOT IS 9 TO 12 FEET TALL.
QUINCY, IS MY HAT AT ABOUT 12 FEET? HOW'S MY HAIR?
BIGFOOT'S SIZE AND WEIGHT MIGHT EXCEED EVEN THE BIGGEST BEARS.
HA, HA! THIS GUY IS NO GRIZZLY!
WE'LL USE STOCK FOOTAGE OF A ROARING BEAR, VERY EXCITING.
YOU'LL EDIT THAT IN LATER. I SEE!
YET UNLIKE BEARS, WHOSE TRAILS, DENS, AND BONES HUNTERS FIND, BIGFOOT REMAINS ELUSIVE!

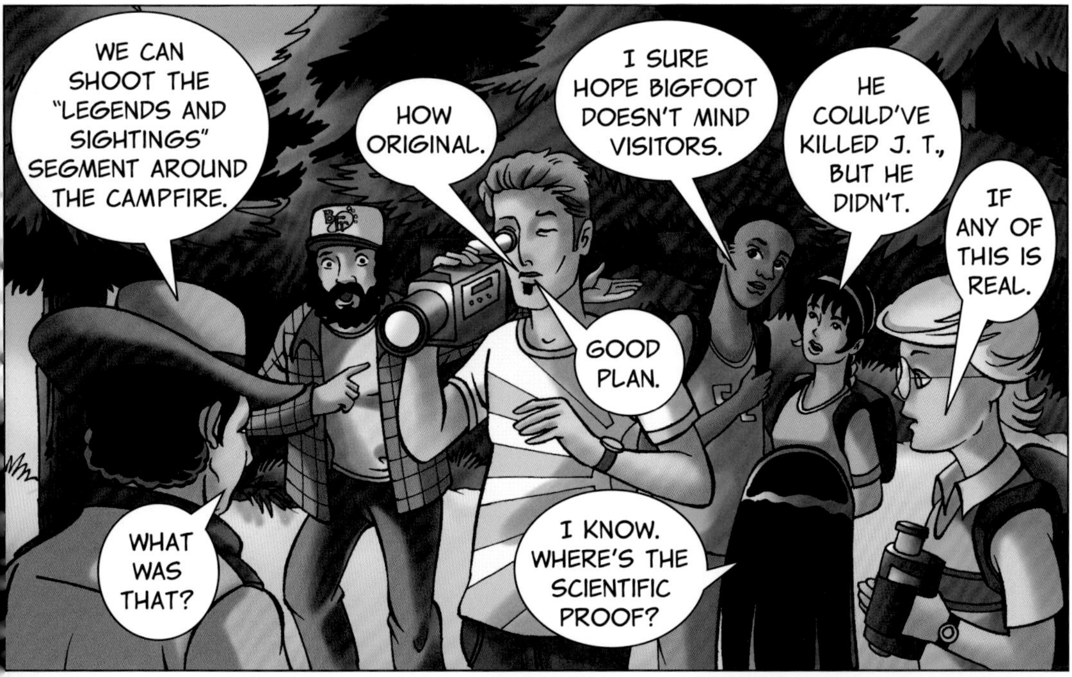
WE CAN SHOOT THE "LEGENDS AND SIGHTINGS" SEGMENT AROUND THE CAMPFIRE.
HOW ORIGINAL.
I SURE HOPE BIGFOOT DOESN'T MIND VISITORS.
HE COULD'VE KILLED J. T., BUT HE DIDN'T.
IF ANY OF THIS IS REAL.
GOOD PLAN.
WHAT WAS THAT?
I KNOW. WHERE'S THE SCIENTIFIC PROOF?

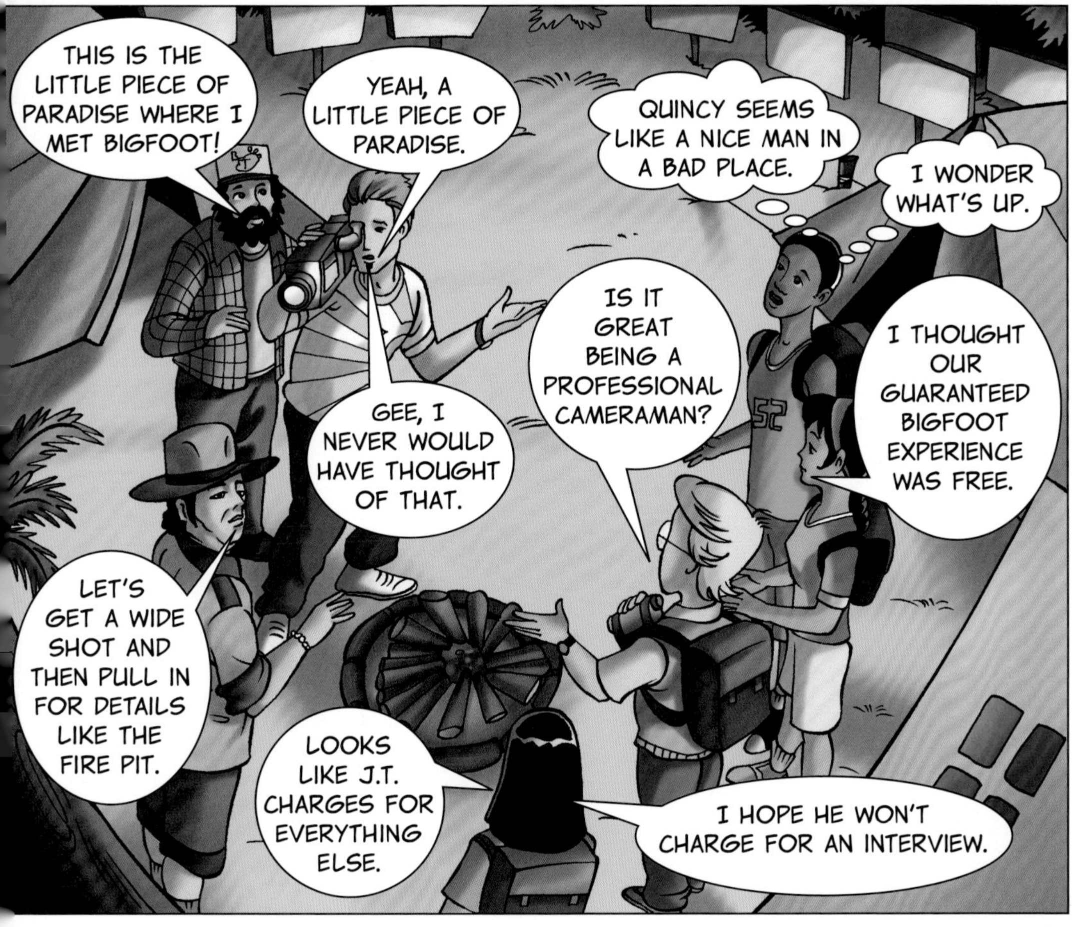
THIS IS THE LITTLE PIECE OF PARADISE WHERE I MET BIGFOOT!
YEAH, A LITTLE PIECE OF PARADISE.
QUINCY SEEMS LIKE A NICE MAN IN A BAD PLACE.
I WONDER WHAT'S UP.
IS IT GREAT BEING A PROFESSIONAL CAMERAMAN?
GEE, I NEVER WOULD HAVE THOUGHT OF THAT.
I THOUGHT OUR GUARANTEED BIGFOOT EXPERIENCE WAS FREE.
LET'S GET A WIDE SHOT AND THEN PULL IN FOR DETAILS LIKE THE FIRE PIT.
LOOKS LIKE J.T. CHARGES FOR EVERYTHING ELSE.
I HOPE HE WON'T CHARGE FOR AN INTERVIEW.

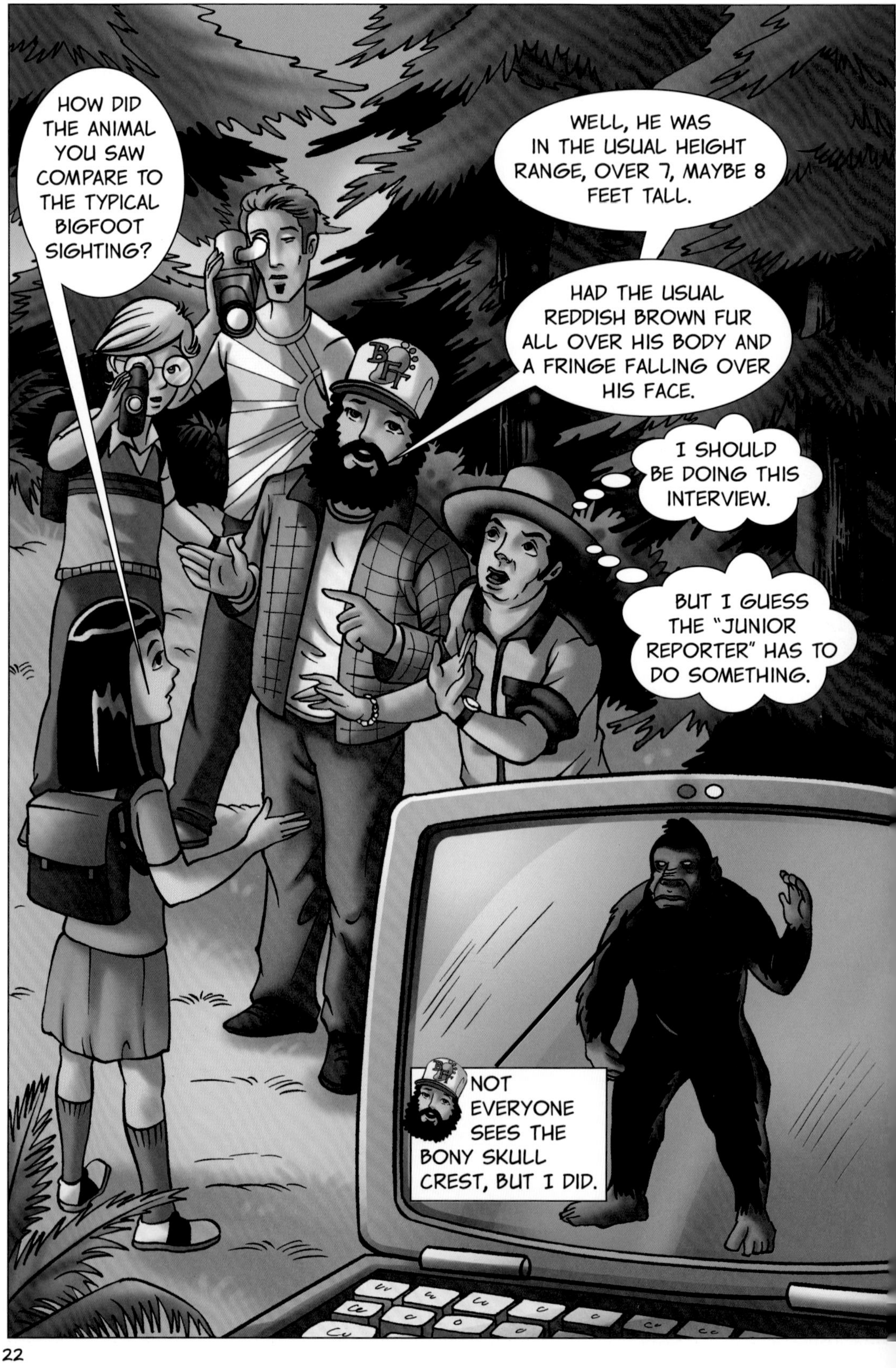
HOW DID THE ANIMAL YOU SAW COMPARE TO THE TYPICAL BIGFOOT SIGHTING?
WELL, HE WAS IN THE USUAL HEIGHT RANGE, OVER 7, MAYBE 8 FEET TALL.
HAD THE USUAL REDDISH BROWN FUR ALL OVER HIS BODY AND A FRINGE FALLING OVER HIS FACE.
I SHOULD BE DOING THIS INTERVIEW.
BUT I GUESS THE "JUNIOR REPORTER" HAS TO DO SOMETHING.
NOT EVERYONE SEES THE BONY SKULL CREST, BUT I DID.

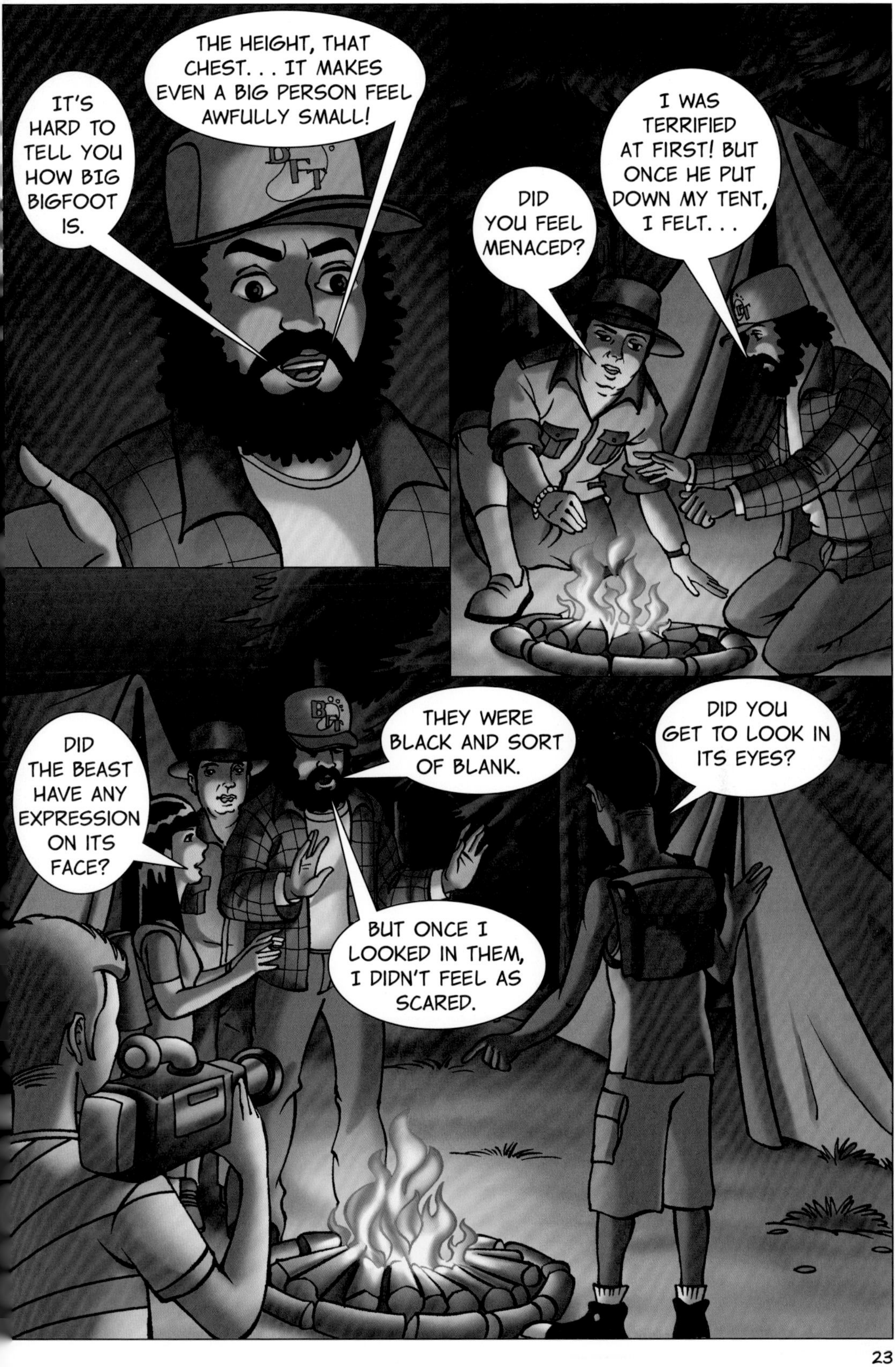
IT'S HARD TO TELL YOU HOW BIG BIGFOOT IS.
THE HEIGHT, THAT CHEST. . . IT MAKES EVEN A BIG PERSON FEEL AWFULLY SMALL!
DID YOU FEEL MENACED?
I WAS TERRIFIED AT FIRST! BUT ONCE HE PUT DOWN MY TENT, I FELT. . .
DID THE BEAST HAVE ANY EXPRESSION ON ITS FACE?
THEY WERE BLACK AND SORT OF BLANK.
BUT ONCE I LOOKED IN THEM, I DIDN'T FEEL AS SCARED.
DID YOU GET TO LOOK IN ITS EYES?

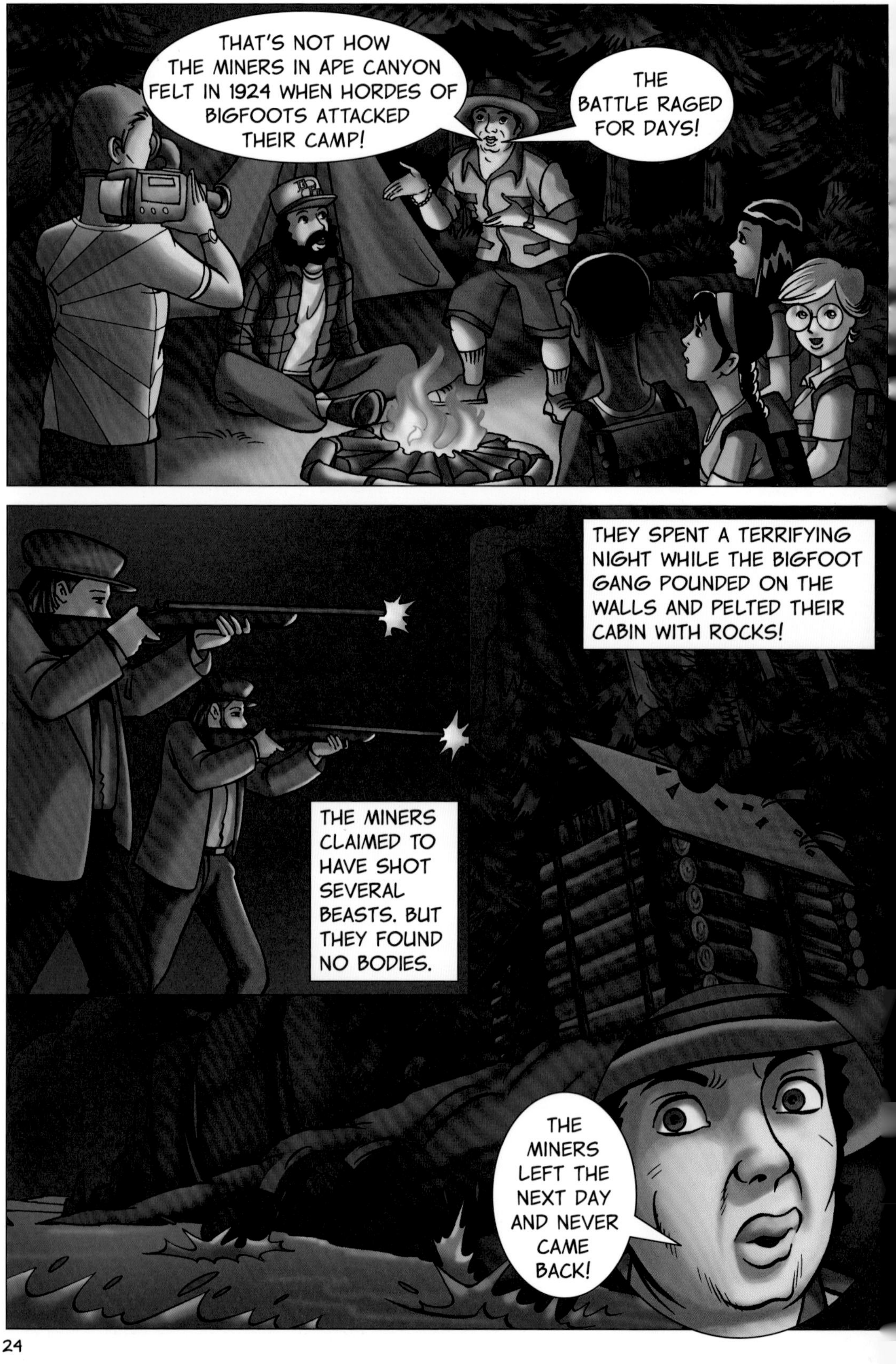
THAT'S NOT HOW THE MINERS IN APE CANYON FELT IN 1924 WHEN HORDES OF BIGFOOTS ATTACKED THEIR CAMP!
THE BATTLE RAGED FOR DAYS!
THEY SPENT A TERRIFYING NIGHT WHILE THE BIGFOOT GANG POUNDED ON THE WALLS AND PELTED THEIR CABIN WITH ROCKS!
THE MINERS CLAIMED TO HAVE SHOT SEVERAL BEASTS. BUT THEY FOUND NO BODIES.
THE MINERS LEFT THE NEXT DAY AND NEVER CAME BACK!

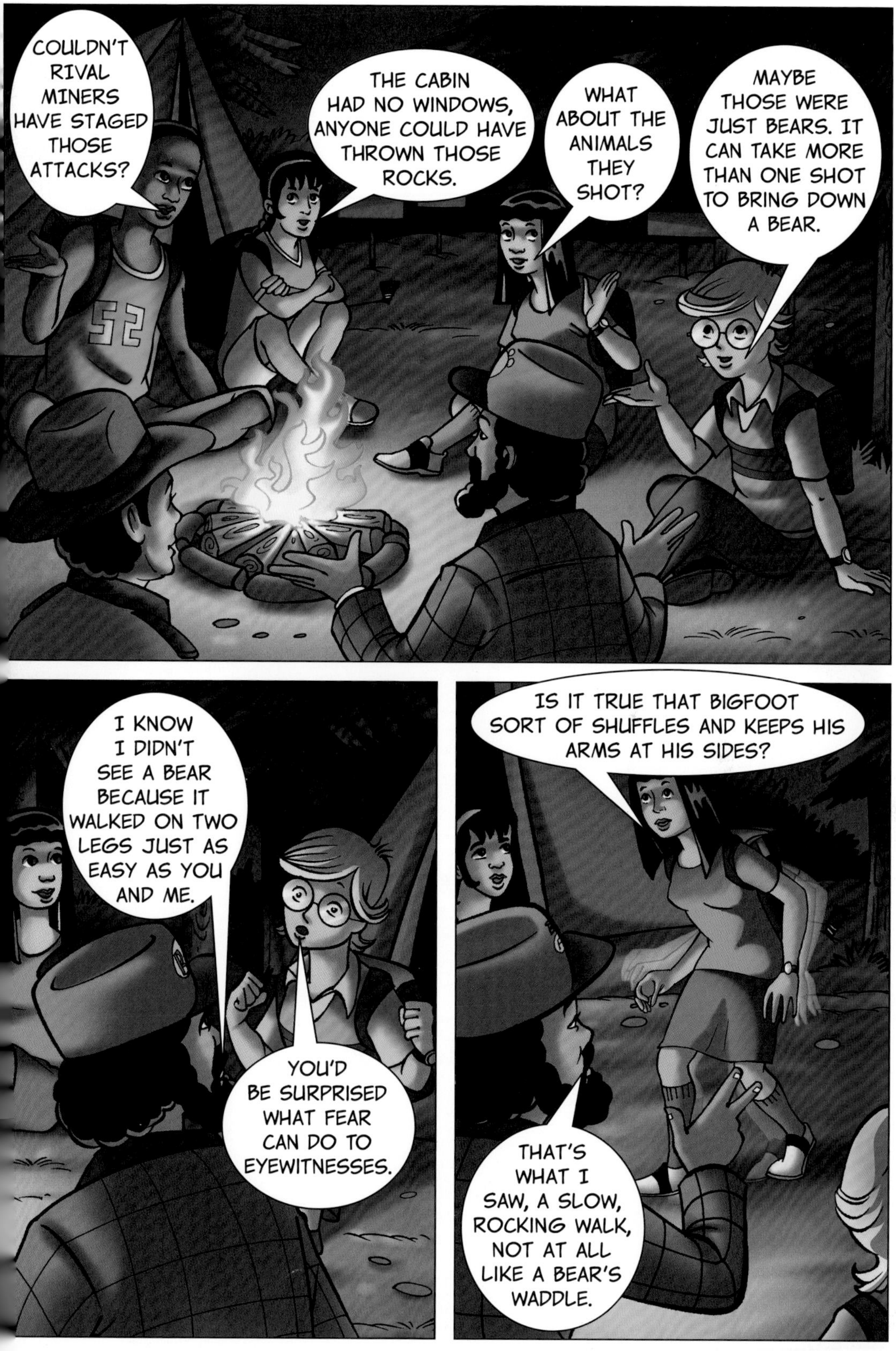
COULDN'T RIVAL MINERS HAVE STAGED THOSE ATTACKS?
THE CABIN HAD NO WINDOWS, ANYONE COULD HAVE THROWN THOSE ROCKS.
WHAT ABOUT THE ANIMALS THEY SHOT?
MAYBE THOSE WERE JUST BEARS. IT CAN TAKE MORE THAN ONE SHOT TO BRING DOWN A BEAR.
I KNOW I DIDN'T SEE A BEAR BECAUSE IT WALKED ON TWO LEGS JUST AS EASY AS YOU AND ME.
YOU'D BE SURPRISED WHAT FEAR CAN DO TO EYEWITNESSES.
IS IT TRUE THAT BIGFOOT SORT OF SHUFFLES AND KEEPS HIS ARMS AT HIS SIDES?
THAT'S WHAT I SAW, A SLOW, ROCKING WALK, NOT AT ALL LIKE A BEAR'S WADDLE.

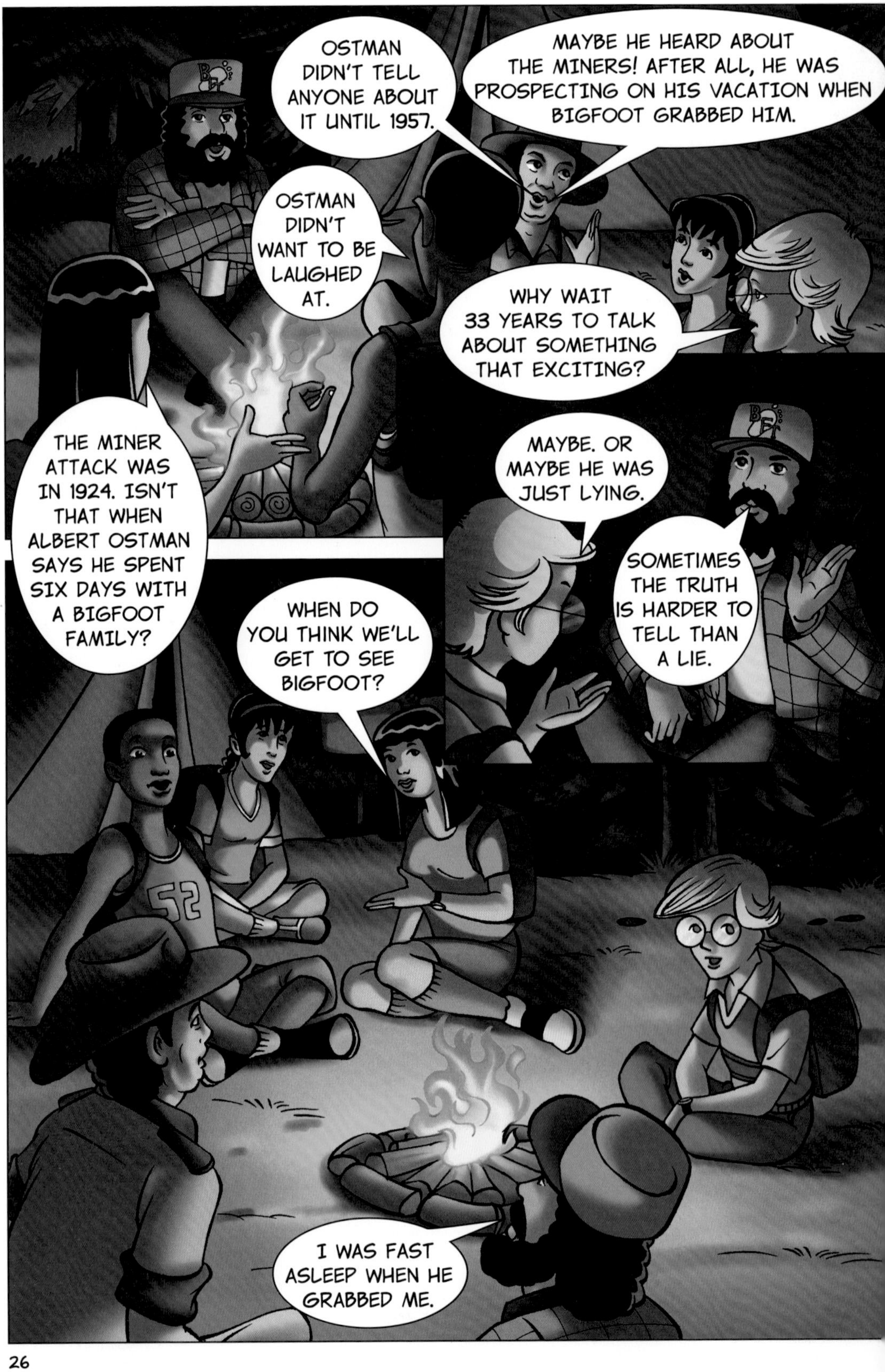
OSTMAN DIDN'T TELL ANYONE ABOUT IT UNTIL 1957.
MAYBE HE HEARD ABOUT THE MINERS! AFTER ALL, HE WAS PROSPECTING ON HIS VACATION WHEN BIGFOOT GRABBED HIM.
OSTMAN DIDN'T WANT TO BE LAUGHED AT.
WHY WAIT 33 YEARS TO TALK ABOUT SOMETHING THAT EXCITING?
THE MINER ATTACK WAS IN 1924. ISN'T THAT WHEN ALBERT OSTMAN SAYS HE SPENT SIX DAYS WITH A BIGFOOT FAMILY?
MAYBE. OR MAYBE HE WAS JUST LYING.
SOMETIMES THE TRUTH IS HARDER TO TELL THAN A LIE.
WHEN DO YOU THINK WE'LL GET TO SEE BIGFOOT?
52
I WAS FAST ASLEEP WHEN HE GRABBED ME.

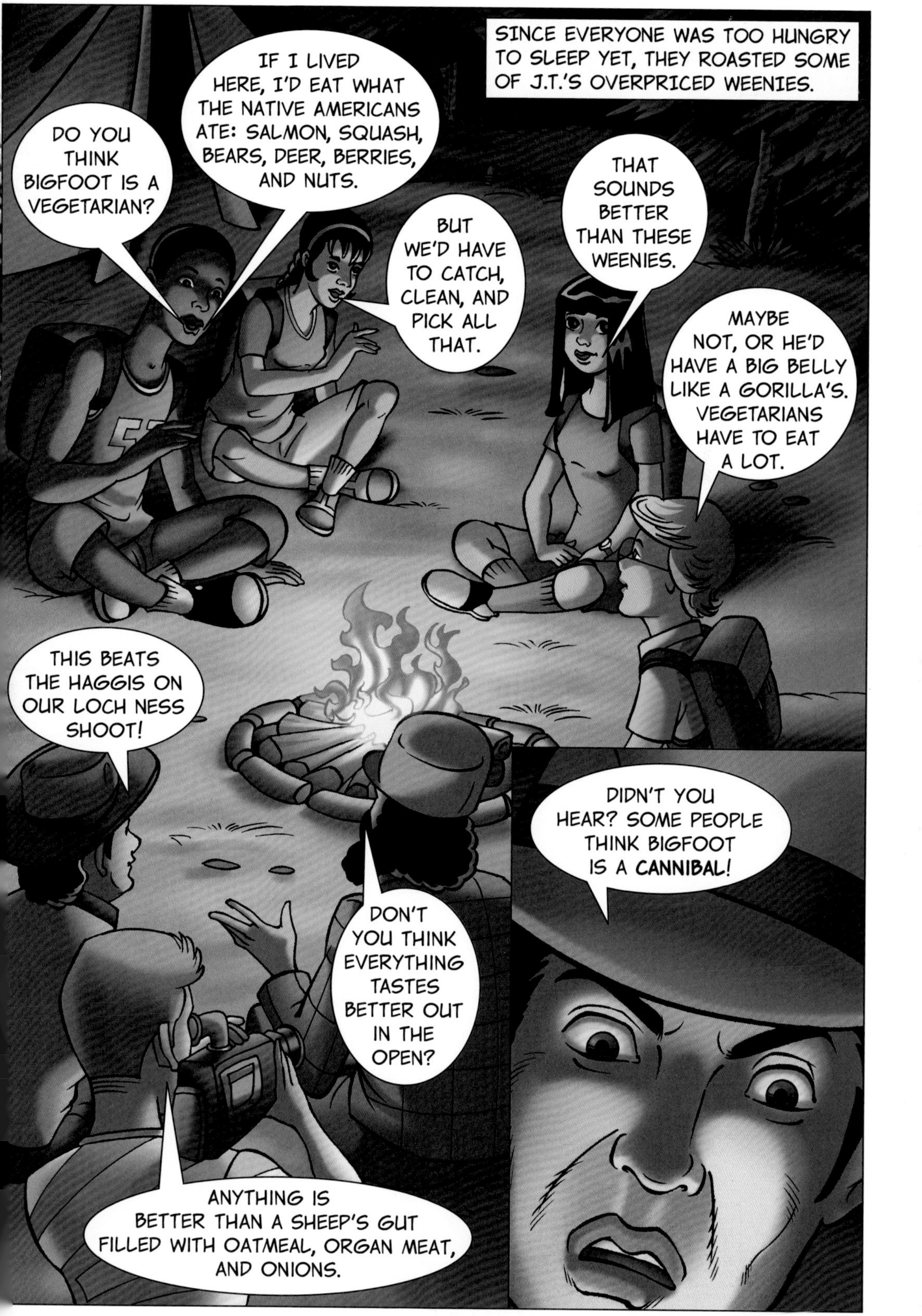
SINCE EVERYONE WAS TOO HUNGRY TO SLEEP YET, THEY ROASTED SOME OF J.T.'S OVERPRICED WEENIES.
DO YOU THINK BIGFOOT IS A VEGETARIAN?
IF I LIVED HERE, I'D EAT WHAT THE NATIVE AMERICANS ATE: SALMON, SQUASH, BEARS, DEER, BERRIES, AND NUTS.
BUT WE'D HAVE TO CATCH, CLEAN, AND PICK ALL THAT.
THAT SOUNDS BETTER THAN THESE WEENIES.
MAYBE NOT, OR HE'D HAVE A BIG BELLY LIKE A GORILLA'S. VEGETARIANS HAVE TO EAT A LOT.
THIS BEATS THE HAGGIS ON OUR LOCH NESS SHOOT!
DON'T YOU THINK EVERYTHING TASTES BETTER OUT IN THE OPEN?
ANYTHING IS BETTER THAN A SHEEP'S GUT FILLED WITH OATMEAL, ORGAN MEAT, AND ONIONS.
DIDN'T YOU HEAR? SOME PEOPLE THINK BIGFOOT IS A CANNIBAL!

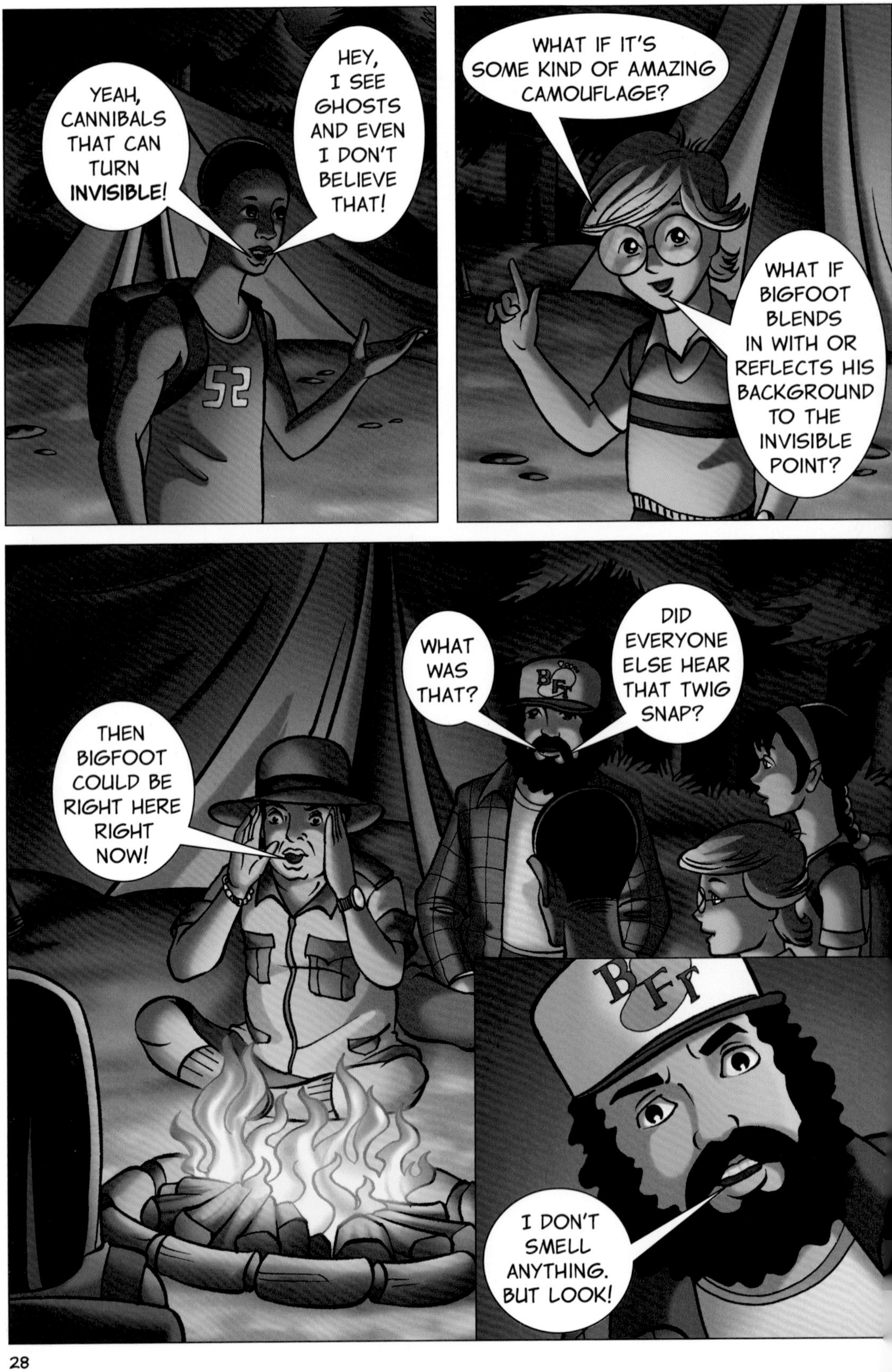
YEAH, CANNIBALS THAT CAN TURN INVISIBLE!
HEY, I SEE GHOSTS AND EVEN I DON'T BELIEVE THAT!
WHAT IF IT'S SOME KIND OF AMAZING CAMOUFLAGE?
WHAT IF BIGFOOT BLENDS IN WITH OR REFLECTS HIS BACKGROUND TO THE INVISIBLE POINT?
THEN BIGFOOT COULD BE RIGHT HERE RIGHT NOW!
WHAT WAS THAT?
DID EVERYONE ELSE HEAR THAT TWIG SNAP?
BFr
I DON'T SMELL ANYTHING. BUT LOOK!

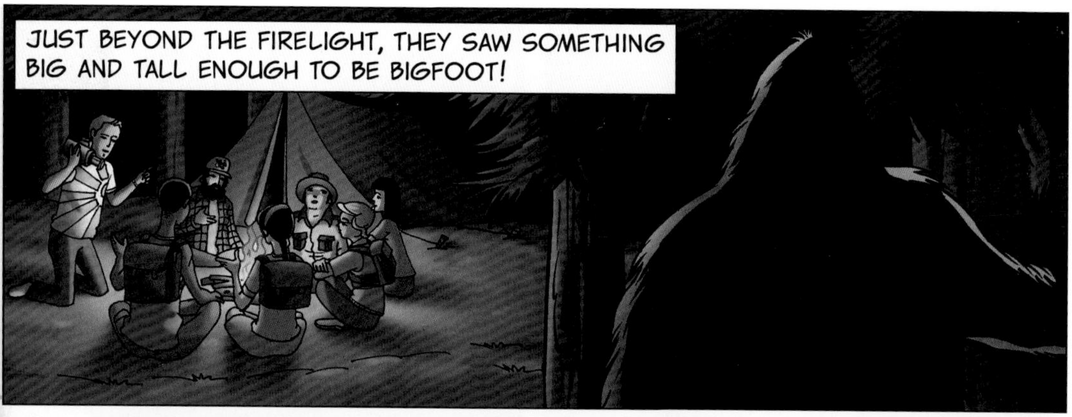
JUST BEYOND THE FIRELIGHT, THEY SAW SOMETHING BIG AND TALL ENOUGH TO BE BIGFOOT!

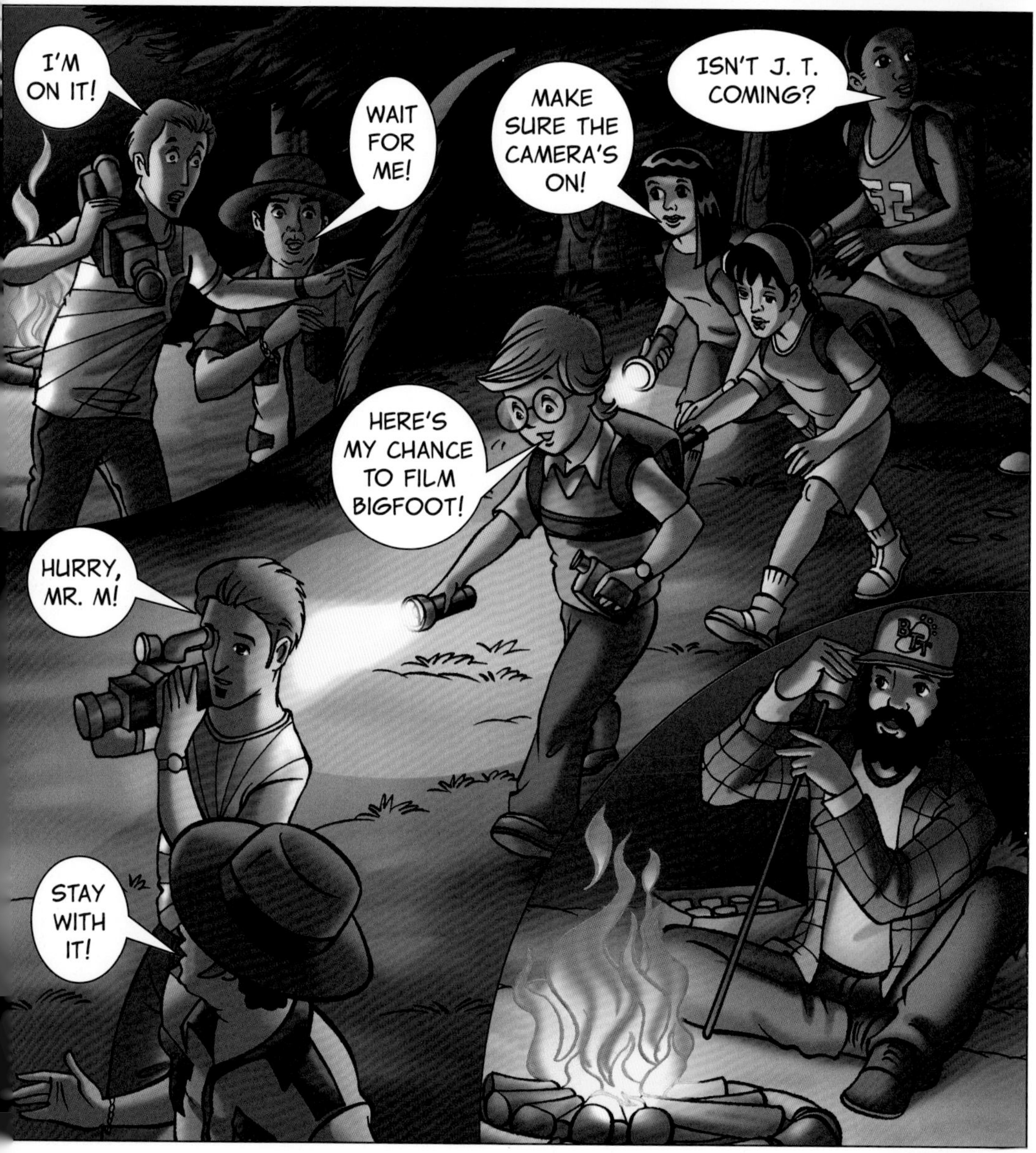
I'M ON IT!
WAIT FOR ME!
MAKE SURE THE CAMERA'S ON!
ISN'T J. T. COMING?
HERE'S MY CHANCE TO FILM BIGFOOT!
HURRY, MR. M!
STAY WITH IT!

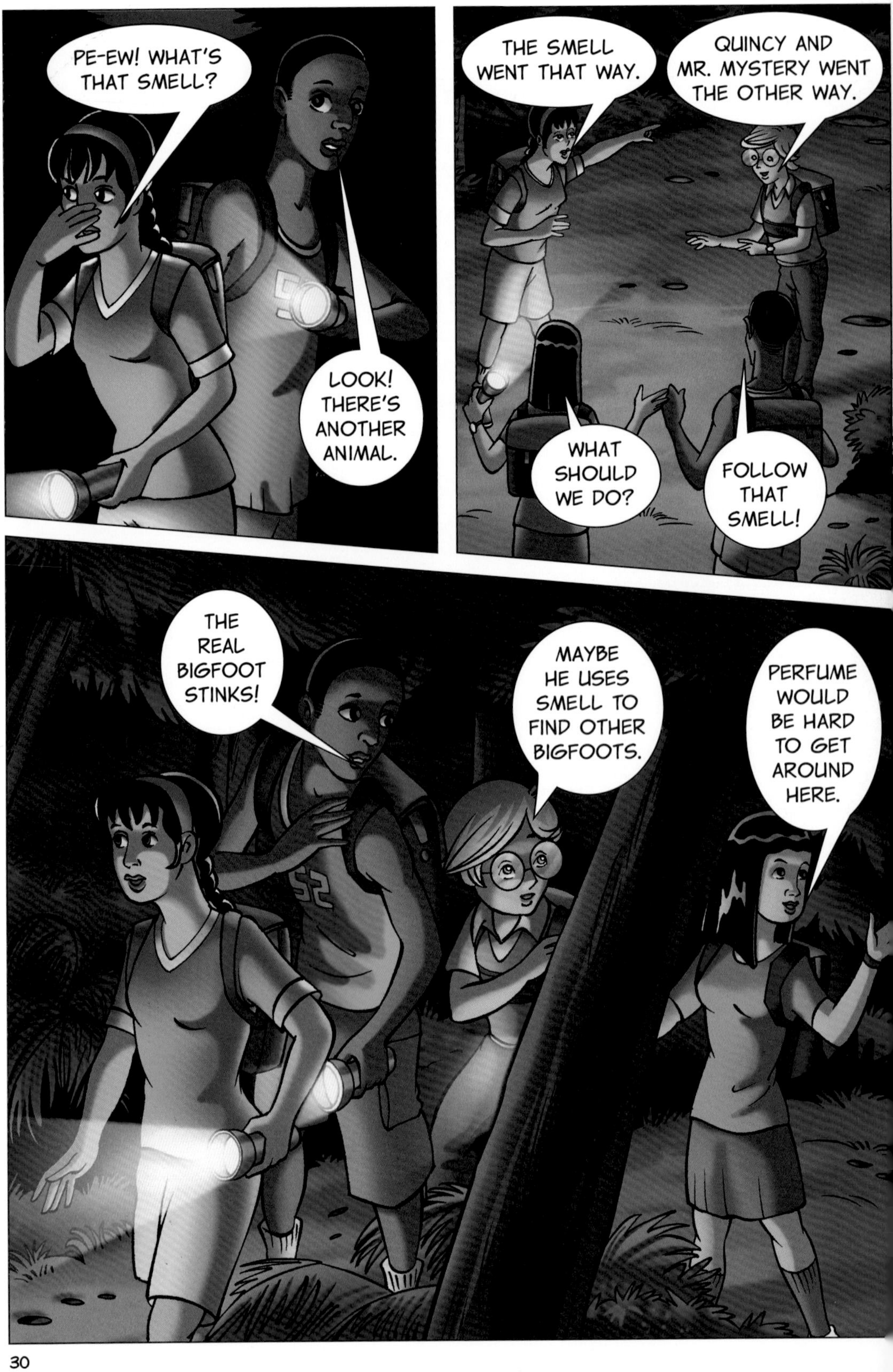
PE-EW! WHAT'S THAT SMELL?
LOOK! THERE'S ANOTHER ANIMAL.
THE SMELL WENT THAT WAY.
QUINCY AND MR. MYSTERY WENT THE OTHER WAY.
WHAT SHOULD WE DO?
FOLLOW THAT SMELL!
THE REAL BIGFOOT STINKS!
MAYBE HE USES SMELL TO FIND OTHER BIGFOOTS.
PERFUME WOULD BE HARD TO GET AROUND HERE.

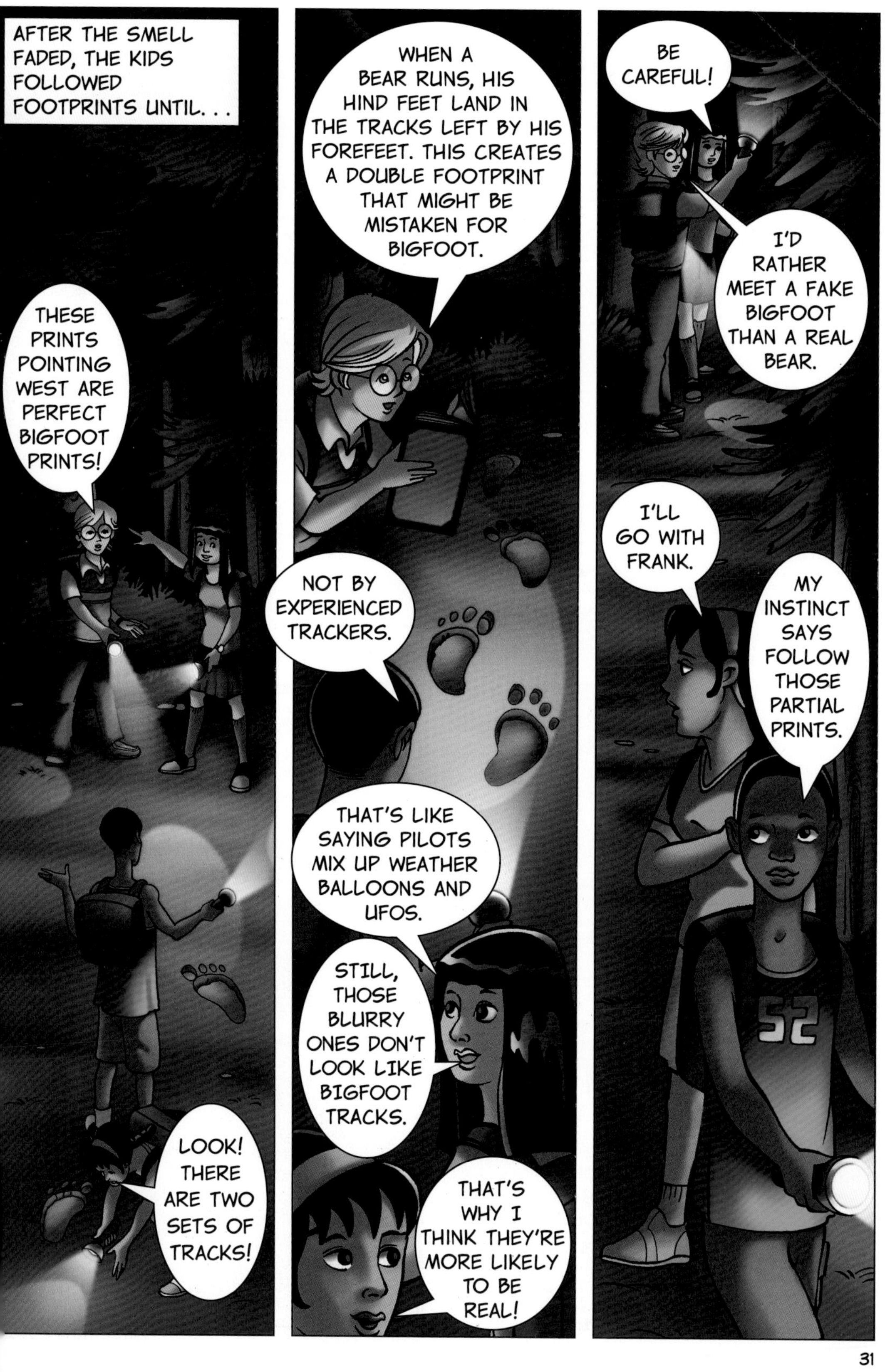
AFTER THE SMELL FADED, THE KIDS FOLLOWED FOOTPRINTS UNTIL. . .
THESE PRINTS POINTING WEST ARE PERFECT BIGFOOT PRINTS!
LOOK! THERE ARE TWO SETS OF TRACKS!
WHEN A BEAR RUNS, HIS HIND FEET LAND IN THE TRACKS LEFT BY HIS FOREFEET. THIS CREATES A DOUBLE FOOTPRINT THAT MIGHT BE MISTAKEN FOR BIGFOOT.
NOT BY EXPERIENCED TRACKERS.
THAT'S LIKE SAYING PILOTS MIX UP WEATHER BALLOONS AND UFOS.
STILL, THOSE BLURRY ONES DON'T LOOK LIKE BIGFOOT TRACKS.
THAT'S WHY I THINK THEY'RE MORE LIKELY TO BE REAL!
BE CAREFUL!
I'D RATHER MEET A FAKE BIGFOOT THAN A REAL BEAR.
I'LL GO WITH FRANK.
MY INSTINCT SAYS FOLLOW THOSE PARTIAL PRINTS.
52

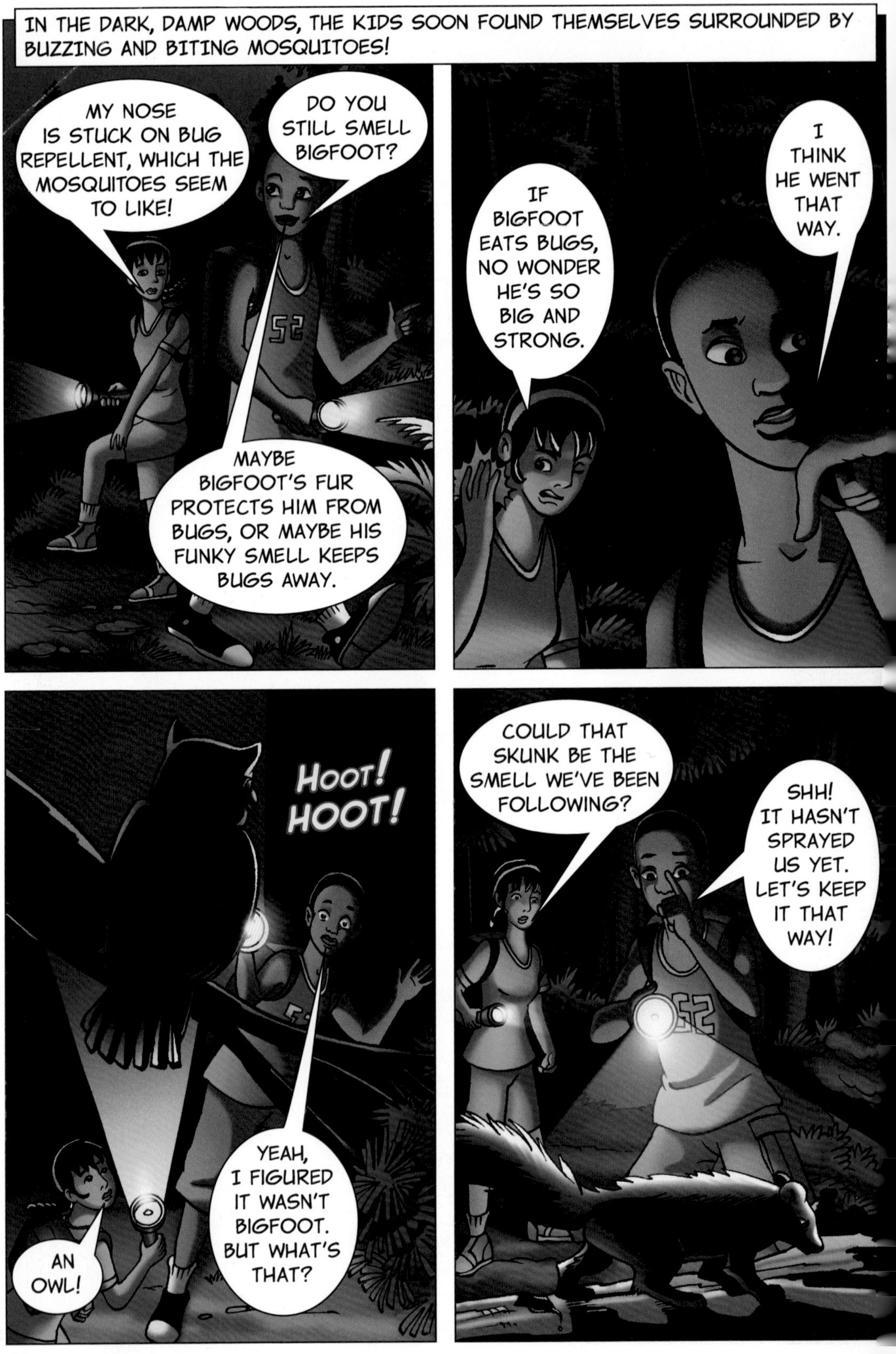
IN THE DARK, DAMP WOODS, THE KIDS SOON FOUND THEMSELVES SURROUNDED BY BUZZING AND BITING MOSQUITOES!
DO YOU STILL SMELL BIGFOOT?
MY NOSE IS STUCK ON BUG REPELLENT, WHICH THE MOSQUITOES SEEM TO LIKE!
MAYBE BIGFOOT'S FUR PROTECTS HIM FROM BUGS, OR MAYBE HIS FUNKY SMELL KEEPS BUGS AWAY.
IF BIGFOOT EATS BUGS, NO WONDER HE'S SO BIG AND STRONG.
I THINK HE WENT THAT WAY.
HOOT! HOOT!
AN OWL!
YEAH, I FIGURED IT WASN'T BIGFOOT. BUT WHAT'S THAT?
COULD THAT SKUNK BE THE SMELL WE'VE BEEN FOLLOWING?
SHH! IT HASN'T SPRAYED US YET. LET'S KEEP IT THAT WAY!

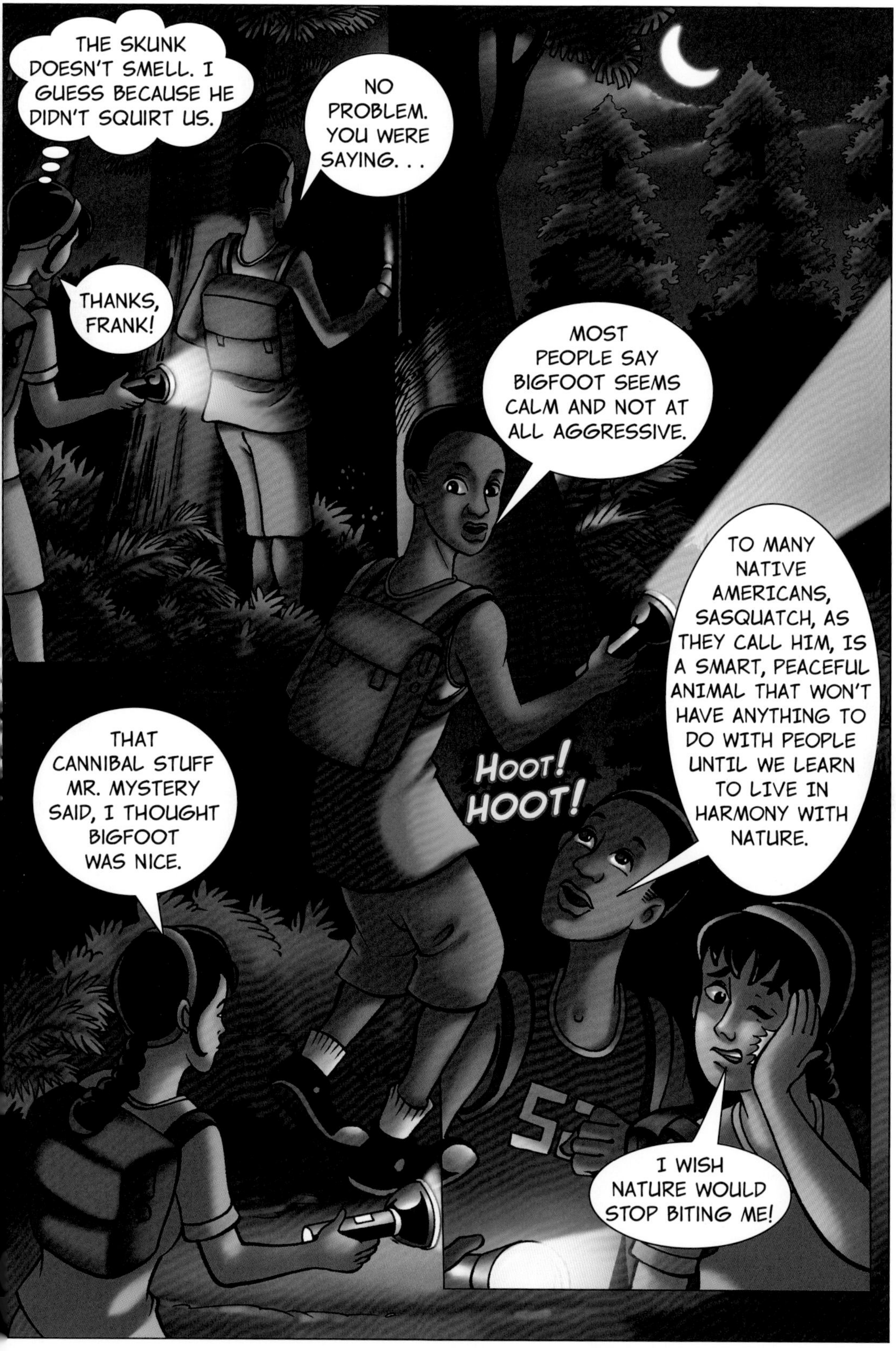
THE SKUNK DOESN'T SMELL. I GUESS BECAUSE HE DIDN'T SQUIRT US.
NO PROBLEM. YOU WERE SAYING. . .
THANKS, FRANK!
MOST PEOPLE SAY BIGFOOT SEEMS CALM AND NOT AT ALL AGGRESSIVE.
TO MANY NATIVE AMERICANS, SASQUATCH, AS THEY CALL HIM, IS A SMART, PEACEFUL ANIMAL THAT WON'T HAVE ANYTHING TO DO WITH PEOPLE UNTIL WE LEARN TO LIVE IN HARMONY WITH NATURE.
THAT CANNIBAL STUFF MR. MYSTERY SAID, I THOUGHT BIGFOOT WAS NICE.
HOOT! HOOT!
I WISH NATURE WOULD STOP BITING ME!

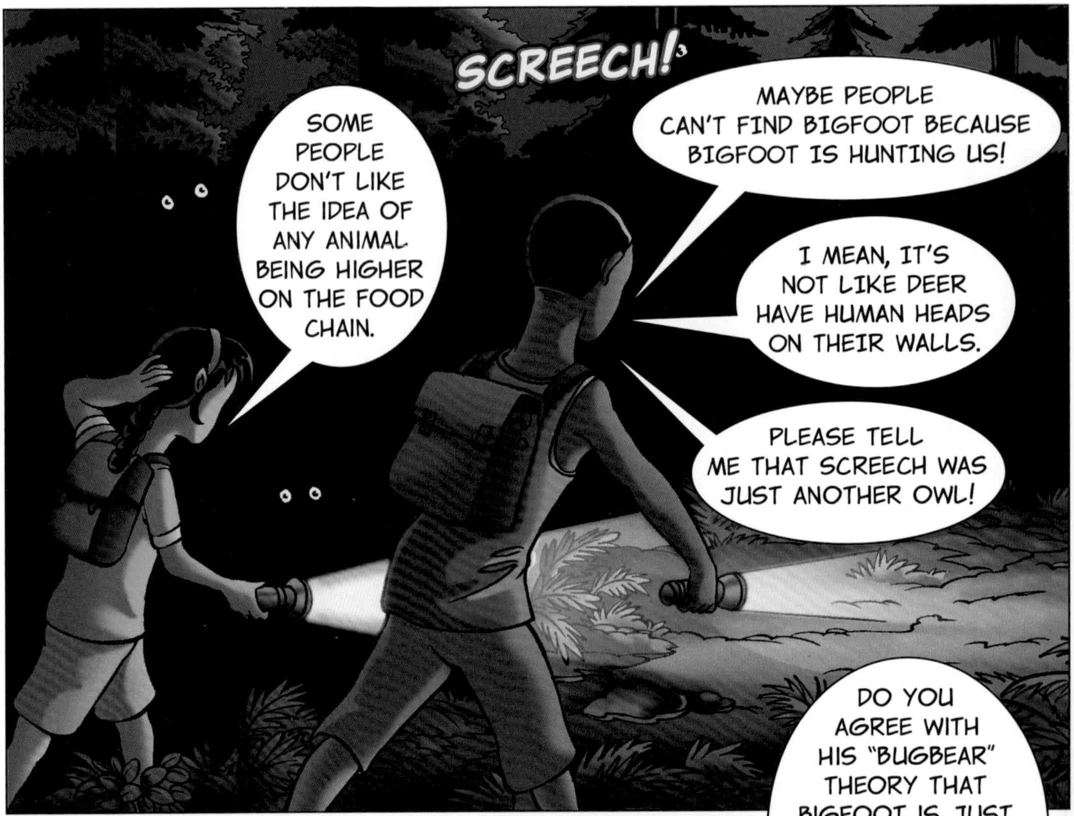
SCREECH!
SOME PEOPLE DON'T LIKE THE IDEA OF ANY ANIMAL BEING HIGHER ON THE FOOD CHAIN.
MAYBE PEOPLE CAN'T FIND BIGFOOT BECAUSE BIGFOOT IS HUNTING US!
I MEAN, IT'S NOT LIKE DEER HAVE HUMAN HEADS ON THEIR WALLS.
PLEASE TELL ME THAT SCREECH WAS JUST ANOTHER OWL!

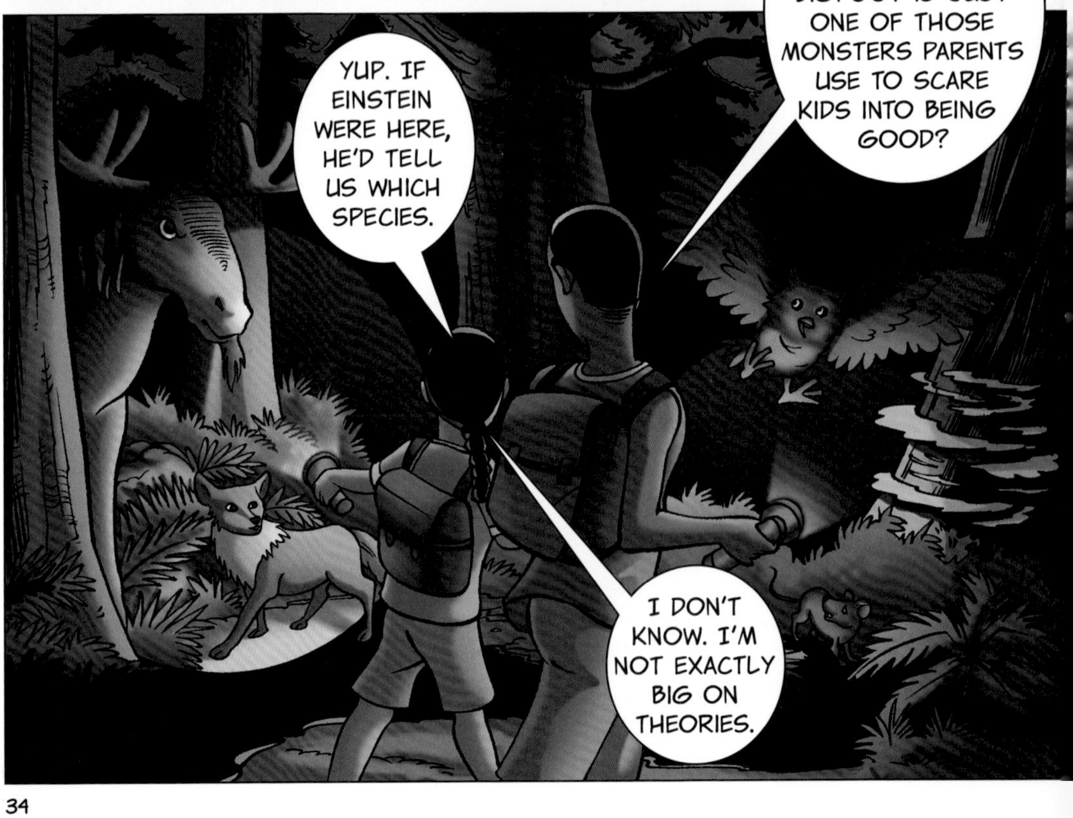
DO YOU AGREE WITH HIS "BUGBEAR" THEORY THAT BIGFOOT IS JUST ONE OF THOSE MONSTERS PARENTS USE TO SCARE KIDS INTO BEING GOOD?
YUP. IF EINSTEIN WERE HERE, HE'D TELL US WHICH SPECIES.
I DON'T KNOW. I'M NOT EXACTLY BIG ON THEORIES.

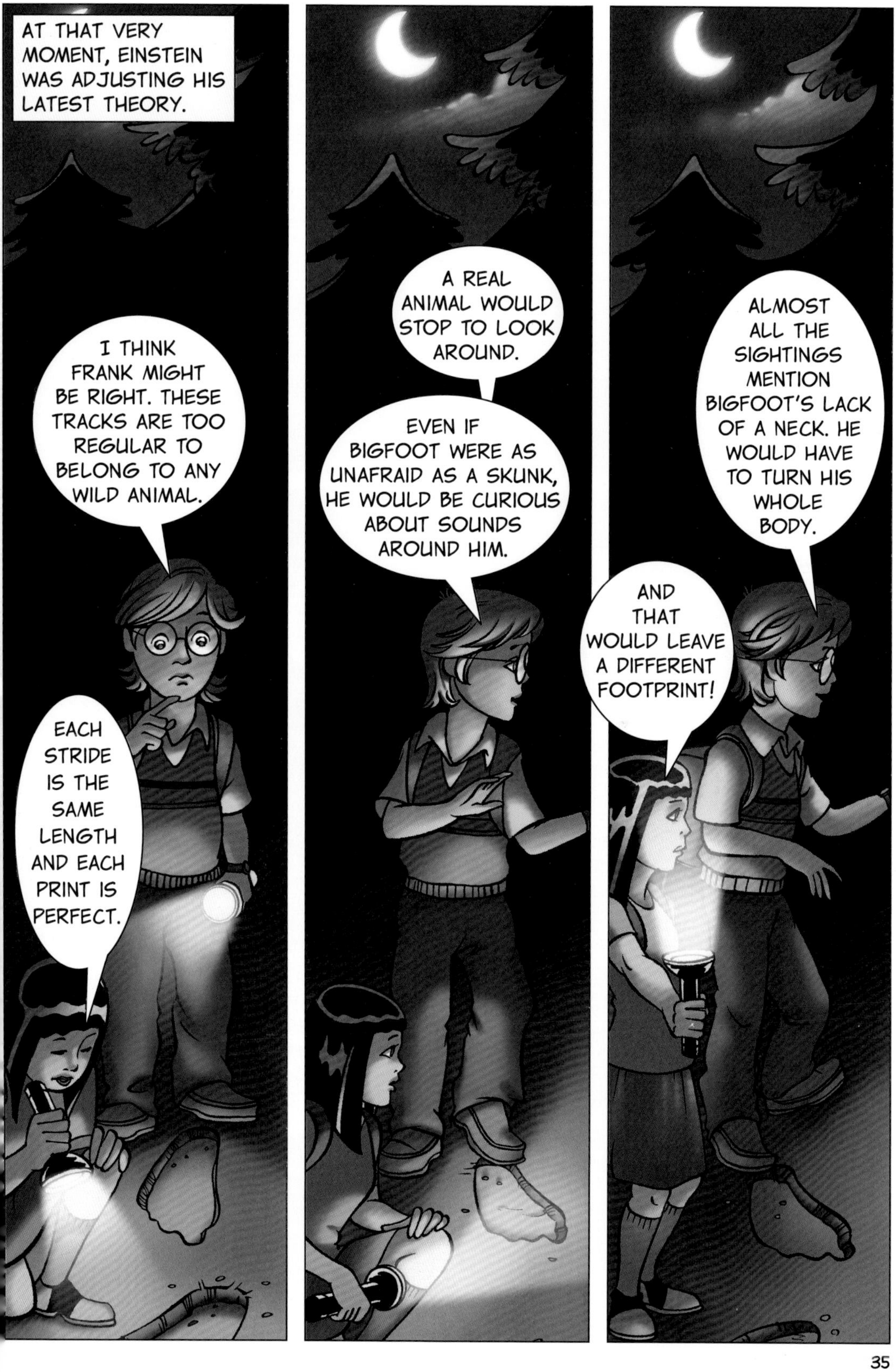
AT THAT VERY MOMENT, EINSTEIN WAS ADJUSTING HIS LATEST THEORY.
I THINK FRANK MIGHT BE RIGHT. THESE TRACKS ARE TOO REGULAR TO BELONG TO ANY WILD ANIMAL.
EACH STRIDE IS THE SAME LENGTH AND EACH PRINT IS PERFECT.
A REAL ANIMAL WOULD STOP TO LOOK AROUND.
EVEN IF BIGFOOT WERE AS UNAFRAID AS A SKUNK, HE WOULD BE CURIOUS ABOUT SOUNDS AROUND HIM.
ALMOST ALL THE SIGHTINGS MENTION BIGFOOT'S LACK OF A NECK. HE WOULD HAVE TO TURN HIS WHOLE BODY.
AND THAT WOULD LEAVE A DIFFERENT FOOTPRINT!

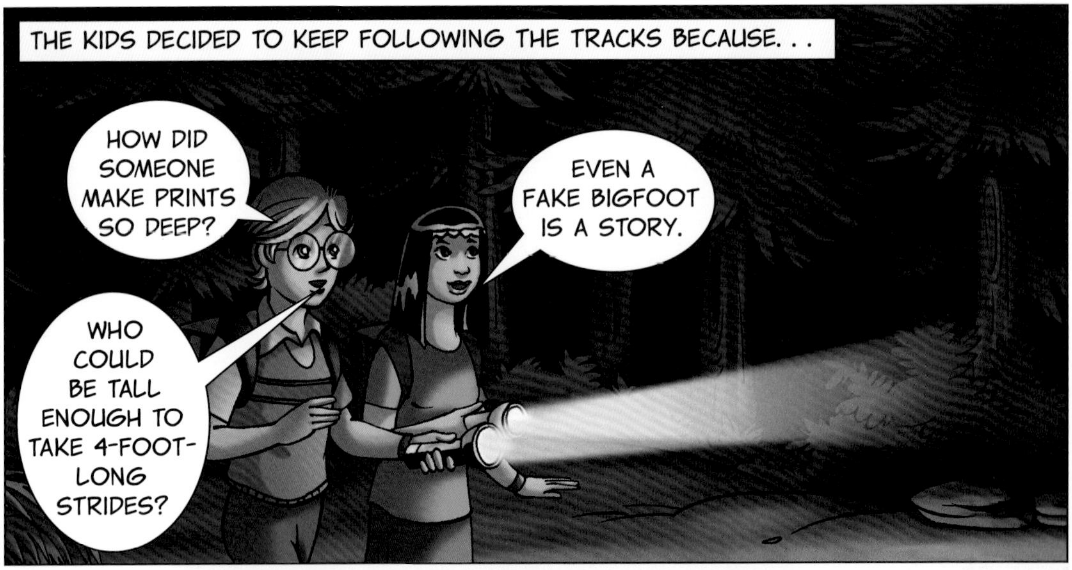
THE KIDS DECIDED TO KEEP FOLLOWING THE TRACKS BECAUSE. . .
HOW DID SOMEONE MAKE PRINTS SO DEEP?
WHO COULD BE TALL ENOUGH TO TAKE 4-FOOT-LONG STRIDES?
EVEN A FAKE BIGFOOT IS A STORY.

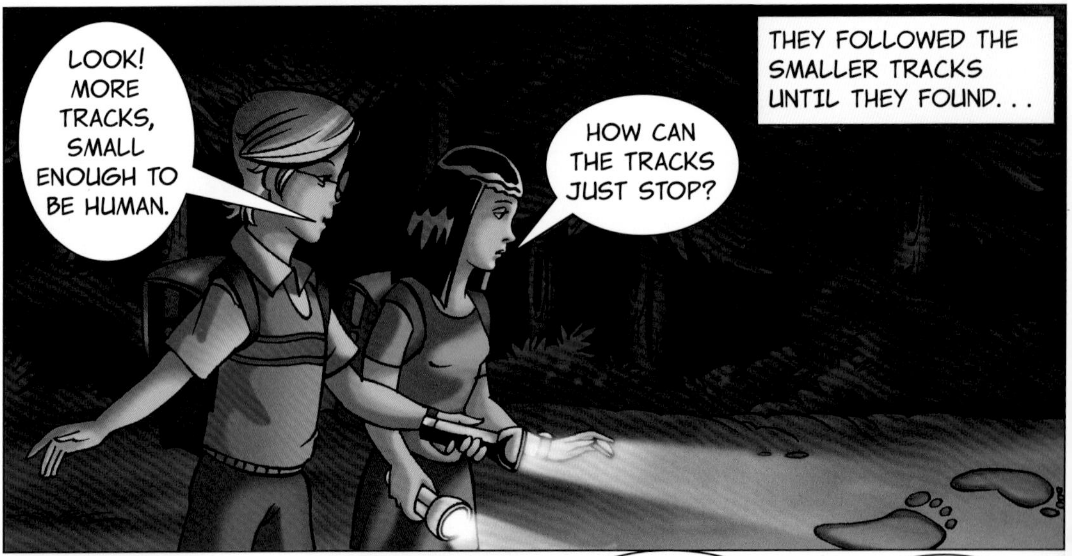
LOOK! MORE TRACKS, SMALL ENOUGH TO BE HUMAN.
THEY FOLLOWED THE SMALLER TRACKS UNTIL THEY FOUND. . .
HOW CAN THE TRACKS JUST STOP?

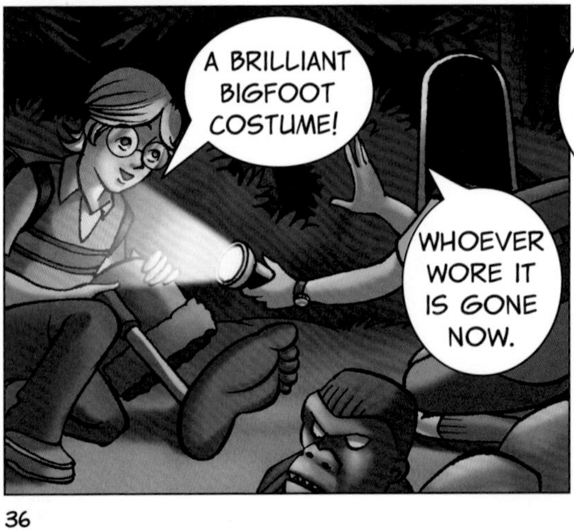
A BRILLIANT BIGFOOT COSTUME!
WHOEVER WORE IT IS GONE NOW.

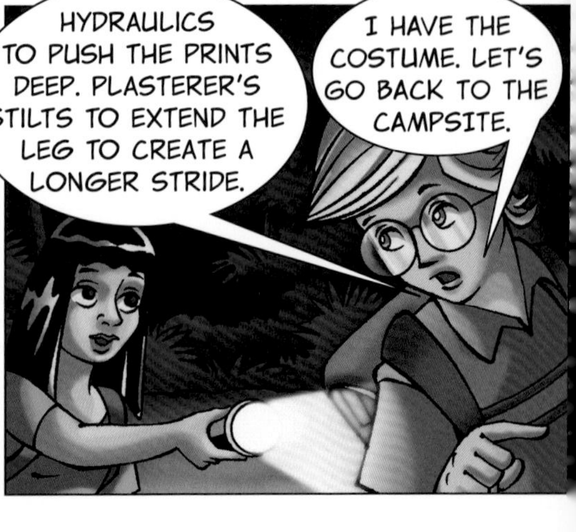
HYDRAULICS TO PUSH THE PRINTS DEEP. PLASTERER'S STILTS TO EXTEND THE LEG TO CREATE A LONGER STRIDE.
I HAVE THE COSTUME. LET'S GO BACK TO THE CAMPSITE.

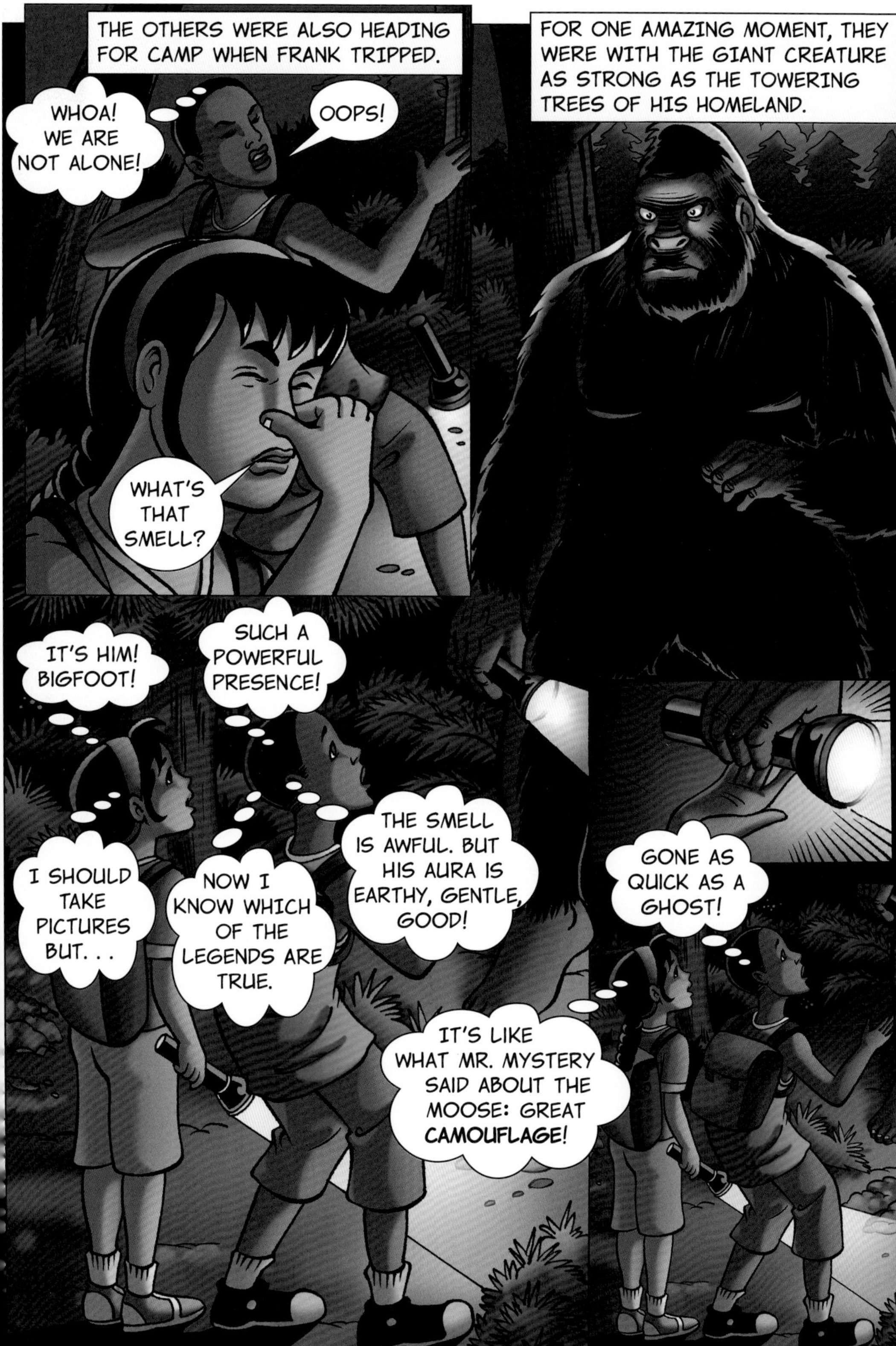
THE OTHERS WERE ALSO HEADING FOR CAMP WHEN FRANK TRIPPED.
WHOA! WE ARE NOT ALONE!
OOPS!
WHAT'S THAT SMELL?
FOR ONE AMAZING MOMENT, THEY WERE WITH THE GIANT CREATURE AS STRONG AS THE TOWERING TREES OF HIS HOMELAND.
IT'S HIM! BIGFOOT!
SUCH A POWERFUL PRESENCE!
I SHOULD TAKE PICTURES BUT. . .
NOW I KNOW WHICH OF THE LEGENDS ARE TRUE.
THE SMELL IS AWFUL. BUT HIS AURA IS EARTHY, GENTLE, GOOD!
GONE AS QUICK AS A GHOST!
IT'S LIKE WHAT MR. MYSTERY SAID ABOUT THE MOOSE: GREAT **CAMOUFLAGE!**

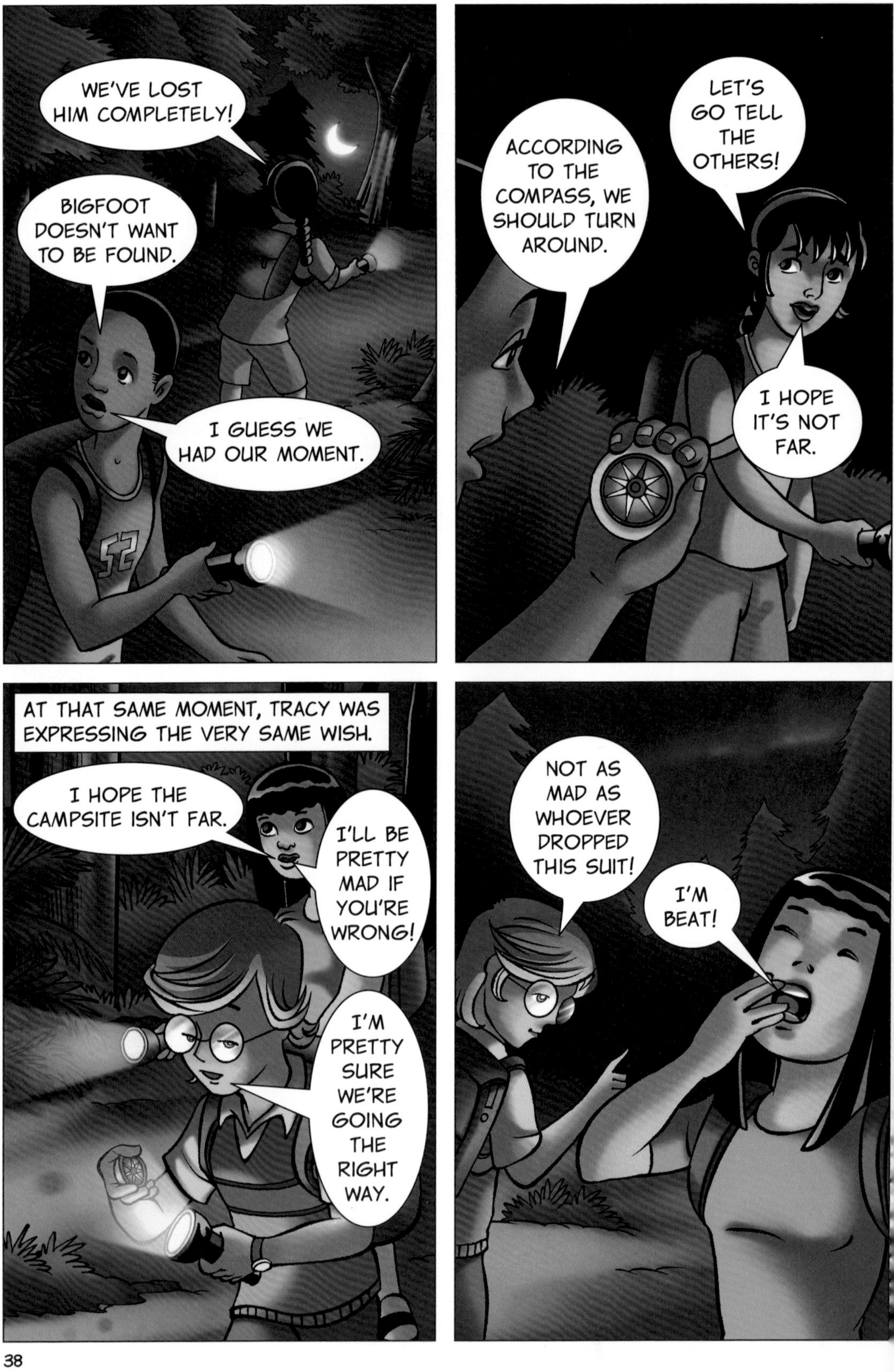
WE'VE LOST HIM COMPLETELY!
BIGFOOT DOESN'T WANT TO BE FOUND.
I GUESS WE HAD OUR MOMENT.
ACCORDING TO THE COMPASS, WE SHOULD TURN AROUND.
LET'S GO TELL THE OTHERS!
I HOPE IT'S NOT FAR.
AT THAT SAME MOMENT, TRACY WAS EXPRESSING THE VERY SAME WISH.
I HOPE THE CAMPSITE ISN'T FAR.
I'LL BE PRETTY MAD IF YOU'RE WRONG!
I'M PRETTY SURE WE'RE GOING THE RIGHT WAY.
NOT AS MAD AS WHOEVER DROPPED THIS SUIT!
I'M BEAT!

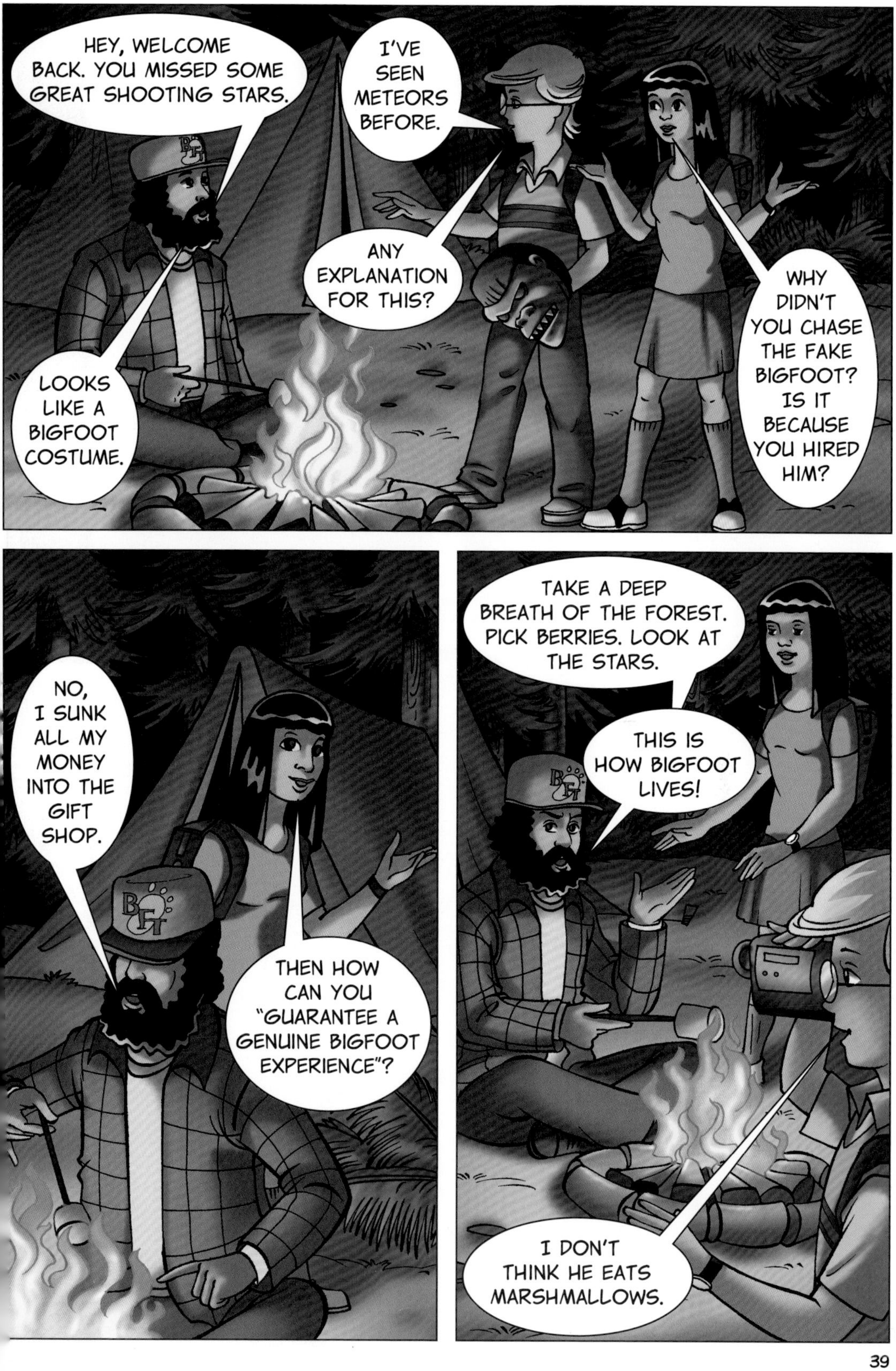
HEY, WELCOME BACK. YOU MISSED SOME GREAT SHOOTING STARS.
I'VE SEEN METEORS BEFORE.
ANY EXPLANATION FOR THIS?
LOOKS LIKE A BIGFOOT COSTUME.
WHY DIDN'T YOU CHASE THE FAKE BIGFOOT? IS IT BECAUSE YOU HIRED HIM?
NO, I SUNK ALL MY MONEY INTO THE GIFT SHOP.
THEN HOW CAN YOU "GUARANTEE A GENUINE BIGFOOT EXPERIENCE"?
TAKE A DEEP BREATH OF THE FOREST. PICK BERRIES. LOOK AT THE STARS.
THIS IS HOW BIGFOOT LIVES!
I DON'T THINK HE EATS MARSHMALLOWS.

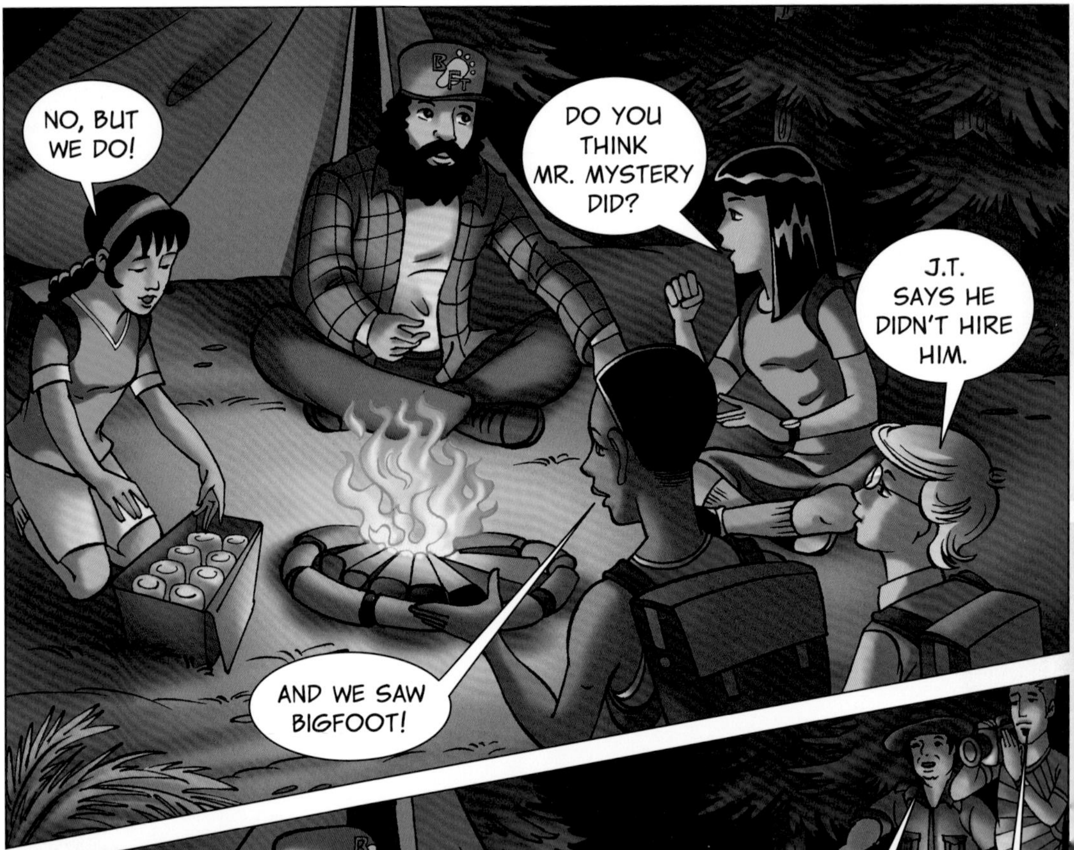
DO YOU THINK MR. MYSTERY DID?
NO, BUT WE DO!
J.T. SAYS HE DIDN'T HIRE HIM.
AND WE SAW BIGFOOT!

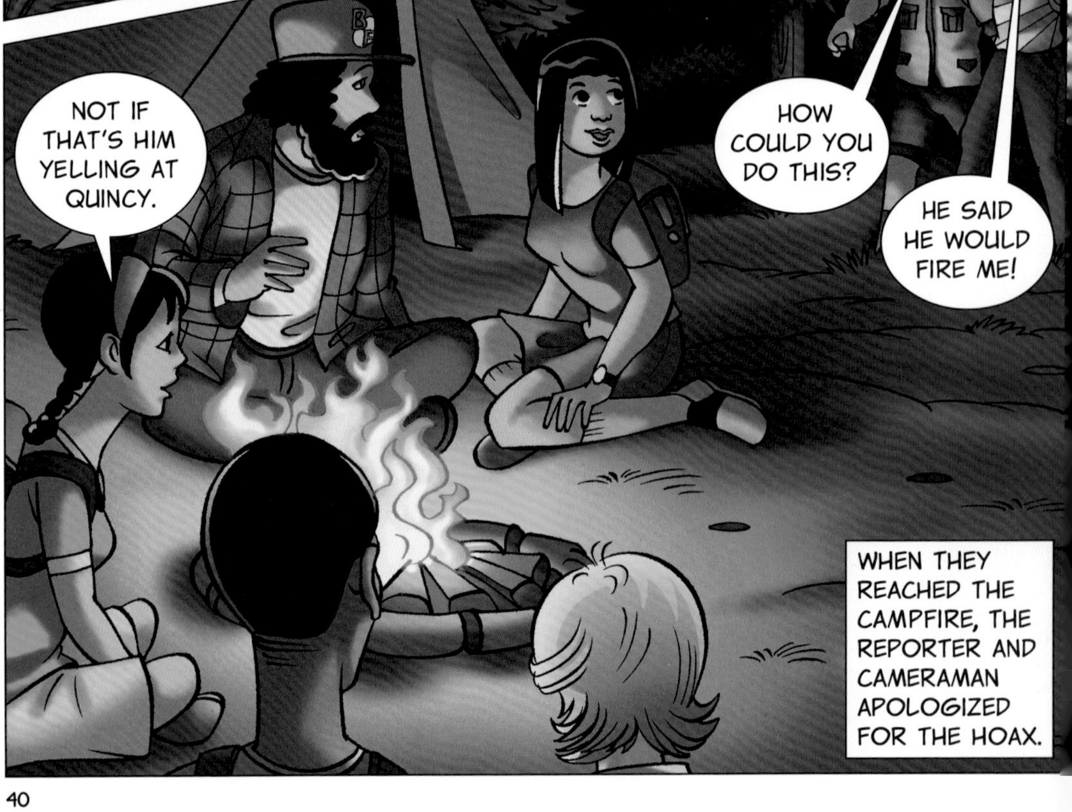
NOT IF THAT'S HIM YELLING AT QUINCY.
HOW COULD YOU DO THIS?
HE SAID HE WOULD FIRE ME!
WHEN THEY REACHED THE CAMPFIRE, THE REPORTER AND CAMERAMAN APOLOGIZED FOR THE HOAX.

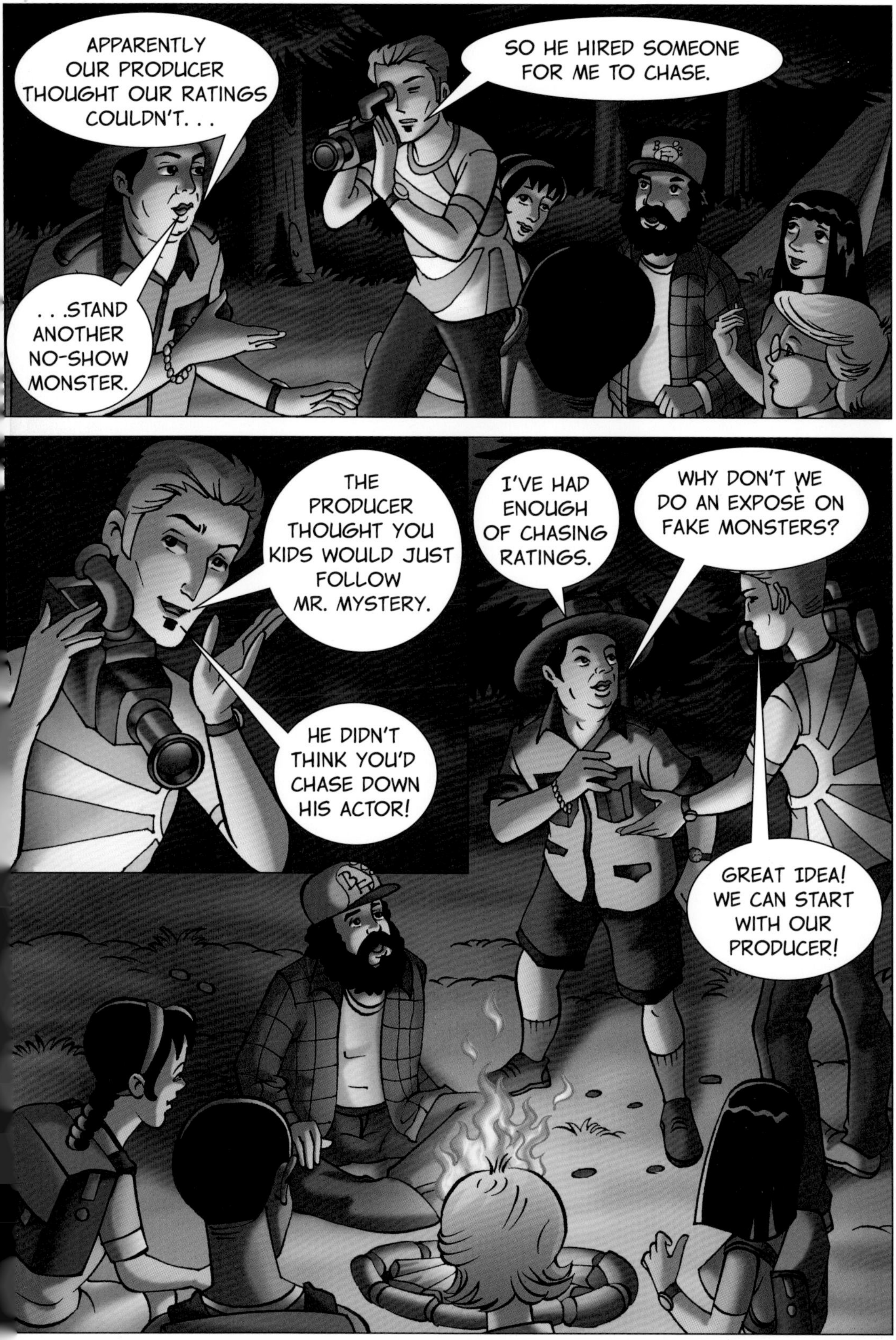
APPARENTLY OUR PRODUCER THOUGHT OUR RATINGS COULDN'T. . .
SO HE HIRED SOMEONE FOR ME TO CHASE.
. . .STAND ANOTHER NO-SHOW MONSTER.
THE PRODUCER THOUGHT YOU KIDS WOULD JUST FOLLOW MR. MYSTERY.
HE DIDN'T THINK YOU'D CHASE DOWN HIS ACTOR!
I'VE HAD ENOUGH OF CHASING RATINGS.
WHY DON'T WE DO AN EXPOSÉ ON FAKE MONSTERS?
GREAT IDEA! WE CAN START WITH OUR PRODUCER!

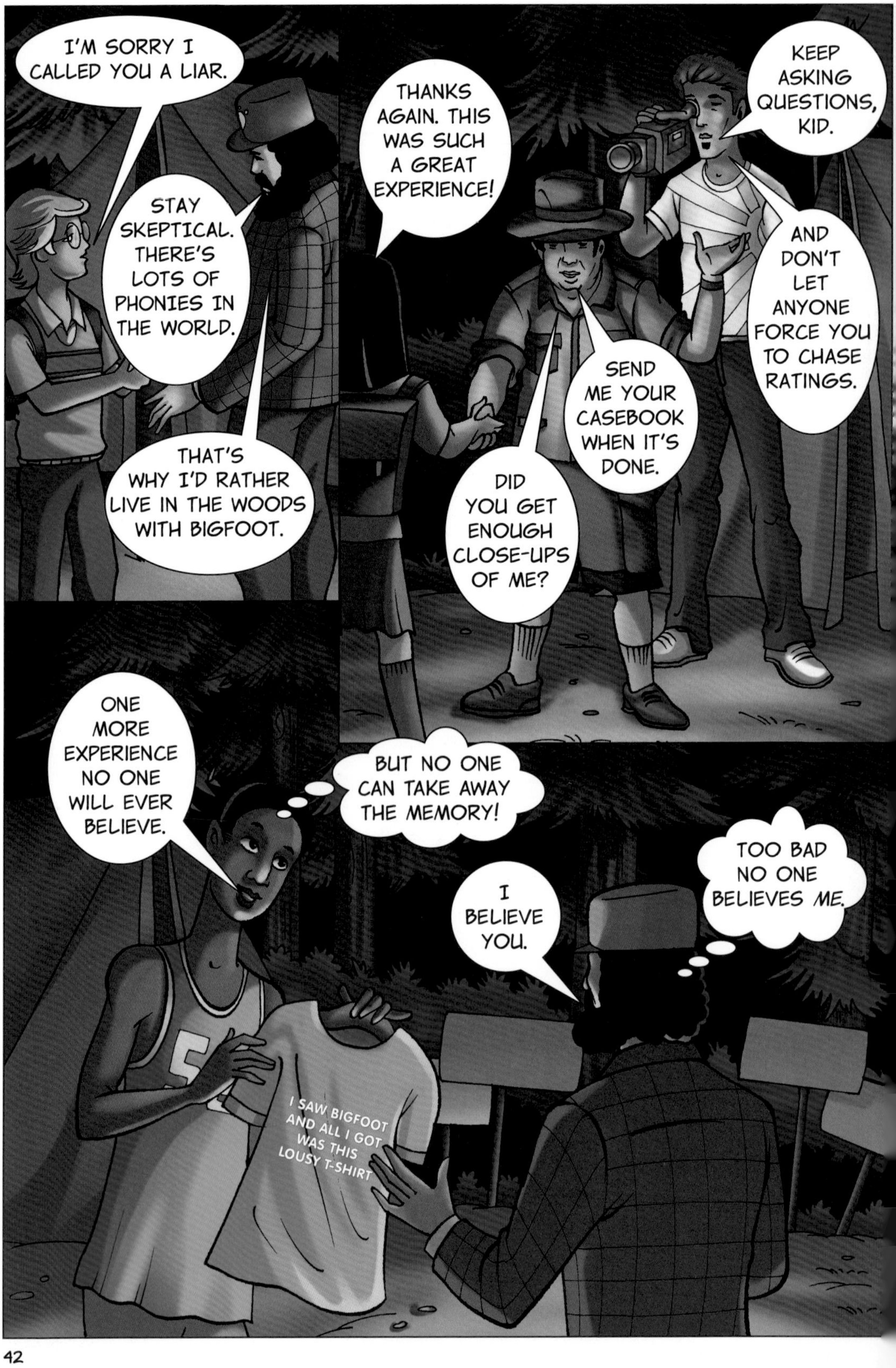
I'M SORRY I CALLED YOU A LIAR.
STAY SKEPTICAL. THERE'S LOTS OF PHONIES IN THE WORLD.
THAT'S WHY I'D RATHER LIVE IN THE WOODS WITH BIGFOOT.
THANKS AGAIN. THIS WAS SUCH A GREAT EXPERIENCE!
KEEP ASKING QUESTIONS, KID.
AND DON'T LET ANYONE FORCE YOU TO CHASE RATINGS.
SEND ME YOUR CASEBOOK WHEN IT'S DONE.
DID YOU GET ENOUGH CLOSE-UPS OF ME?
ONE MORE EXPERIENCE NO ONE WILL EVER BELIEVE.
BUT NO ONE CAN TAKE AWAY THE MEMORY!
TOO BAD NO ONE BELIEVES ME.
I BELIEVE YOU.
I SAW BIGFOOT AND ALL I GOT WAS THIS LOUSY T-SHIRT

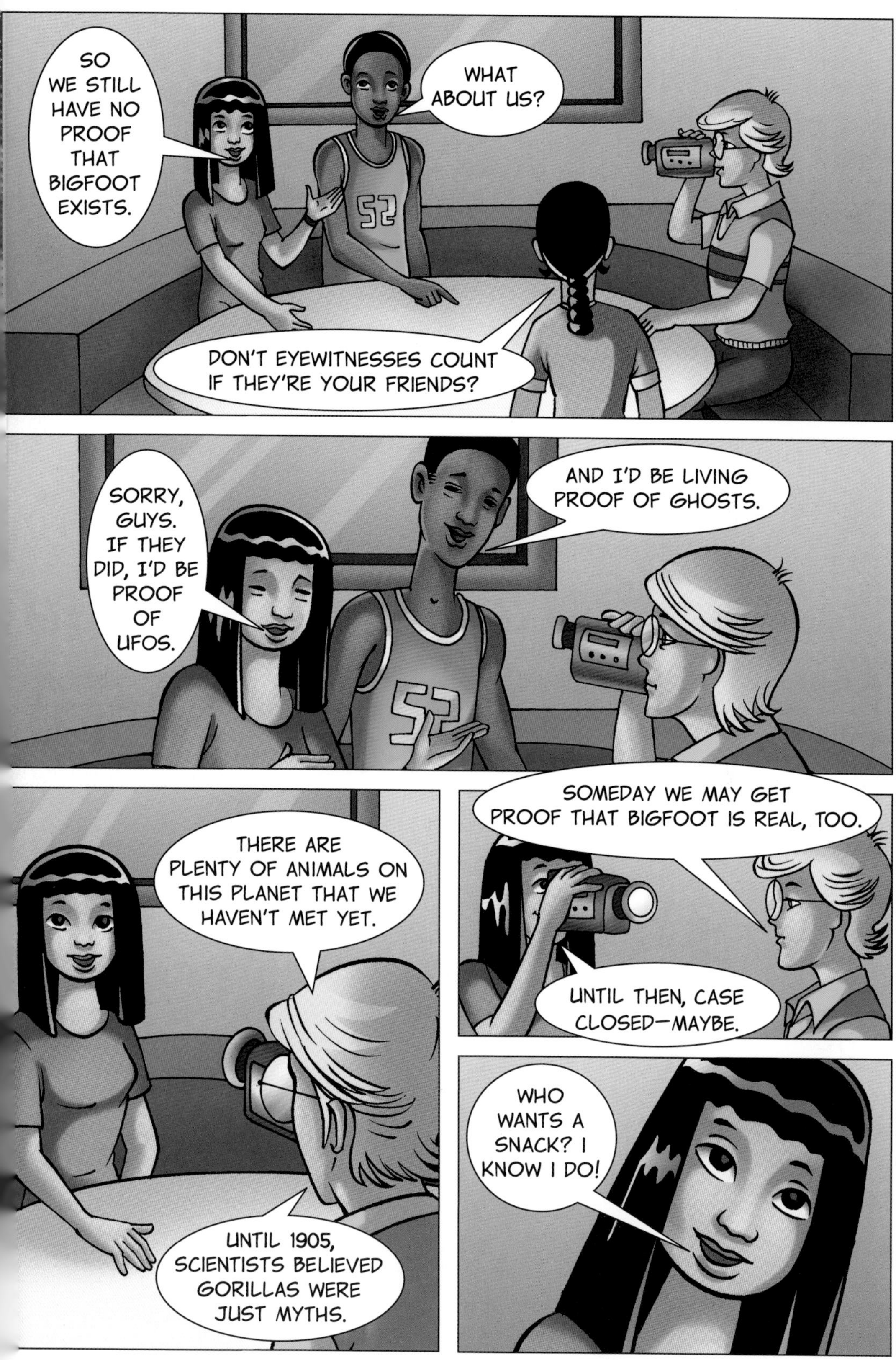
SO WE STILL HAVE NO PROOF THAT BIGFOOT EXISTS.
WHAT ABOUT US?
DON'T EYEWITNESSES COUNT IF THEY'RE YOUR FRIENDS?
SORRY, GUYS. IF THEY DID, I'D BE PROOF OF UFOS.
AND I'D BE LIVING PROOF OF GHOSTS.
THERE ARE PLENTY OF ANIMALS ON THIS PLANET THAT WE HAVEN'T MET YET.
UNTIL 1905, SCIENTISTS BELIEVED GORILLAS WERE JUST MYTHS.
SOMEDAY WE MAY GET PROOF THAT BIGFOOT IS REAL, TOO.
UNTIL THEN, CASE CLOSED—MAYBE.
WHO WANTS A SNACK? I KNOW I DO!

FACT FILE

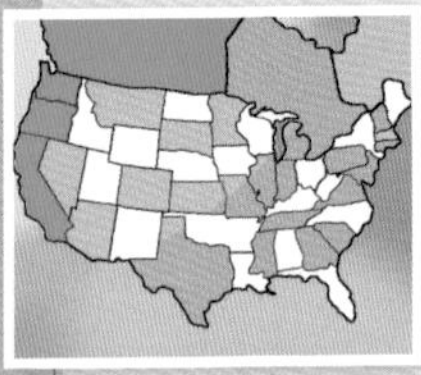

Pacific Northwest: An area that encompasses the northwestern United States and part of western Canada. It includes Washington State, Oregon, and parts of Northern California. Thousands of square miles are nearly completely free of people most of the time. It is the location of most Bigfoot sightings.

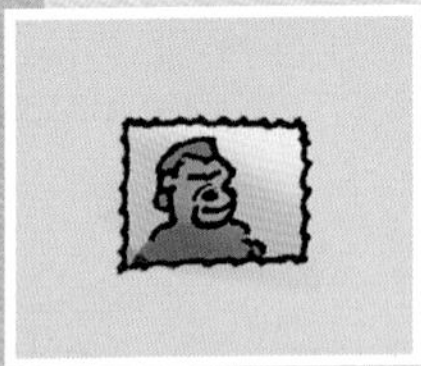

Yeti: The name used by natives of the Himalayan Mountains for the wild, furry manlike beast that leaves large footprints in the snow.

FACT FILE

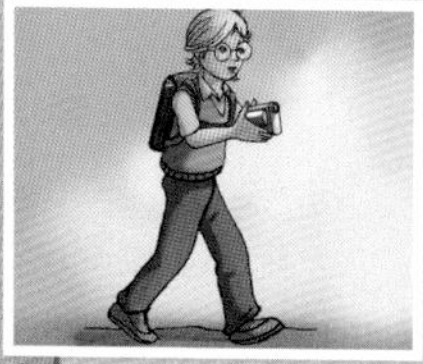

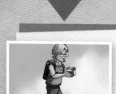

Biped: From the Latin, *bi* meaning "two" and *pedis* meaning "foot;" an animal in the habit of walking on two legs.

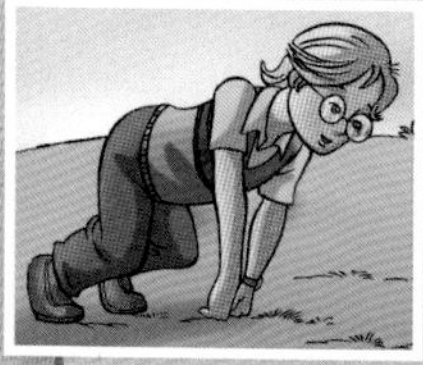

Quadruped: From the Latin, *quadru* meaning "four" and *pedis* meaning "foot;" any animal that walks on four feet most of the time.

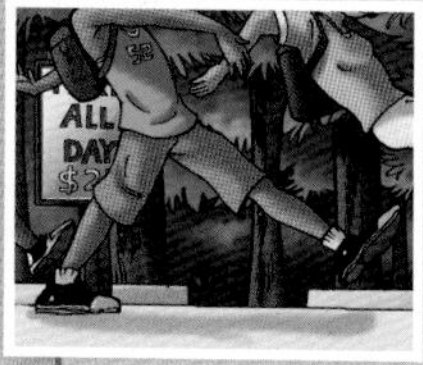
ALL
DAY

Stride: The distance covered by a full step. Trackers know an animal's stride and gait, its style of walking or running. Bigfoot has the stride of a very tall animal. Some estimates put it taller than 11 feet (3.35 m)!

FACT FILE

The Patterson film: The best film of Bigfoot so far. It's about 20 feet of 16-mm film showing a female Bigfoot walking. It was filmed by Roger Patterson in 1967 in Bluff Creek valley, in northern California.

Stilts: Long post or poles used to hold things or people above the ground. Construction workers use **plasterer's stilts** to spread plaster on tall walls without having to keep moving a ladder. Stilts would give a fake Bigfoot an artificially long stride.

Camouflage: From the French *camoufler* meaning "to disguise;" the use of colors and/or patterns to blend in with the background; many animals use camouflage to hide from predators just as soldiers wear special camouflage clothes and makeup to hide from the enemy.

Find Out for Yourself

Tracy was too busy chasing through the woods to cover every aspect of Bigfoot. Dig up the truth about these topics to create your own casebook. What can you find out about?

- Albert Ostman's story
- Abominable snowmen
- Sasquatch and Native American legends
- Animal tracks
- Giganthropithecus
- The miners at Ape Canyon
- Wildman legends

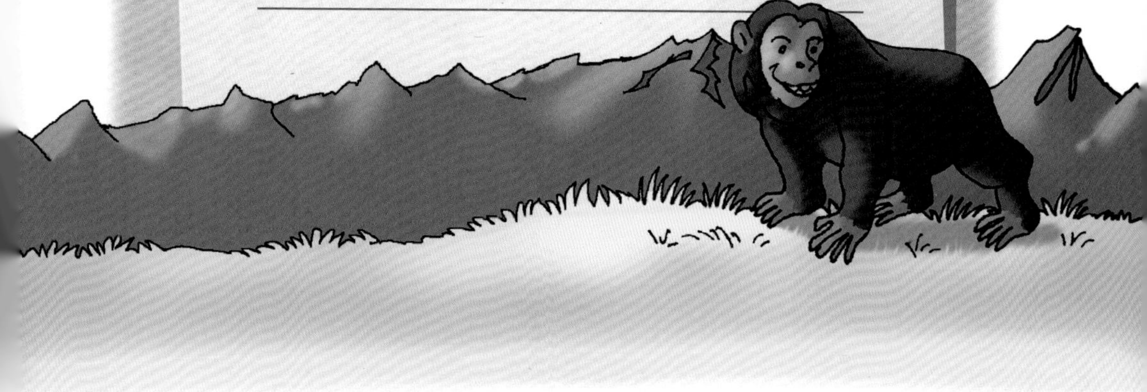

Web Sites

To ensure the currency and safety of recommended Internet links, Windmill maintains and updates an online list of sites related to the subject of this book. To access this list of Web sites, please go to **www.windmillbks.com/weblinks** and select this book's title.

About the Author/Artist

Justine and Ron Fontes met at a publishing house in New York City, where he worked for the comic book department and she was an editorial assistant in children's books. Together, they have written over 500 children's books, in every format from board books to historical novels. They live in Maine, where they continue their work in writing and comics and publish a newsletter, *critter news*.

For more great fiction and nonfiction, go to www.windmillbooks.com